The Witch of Wapping

by Rebecca J. Allred and Alan M. Clark

IFD Publishing, P.O. Box 41281, Eugene, Oregon 97404 U.S.A.
www.ifdpublishing.com

The Witch of Wapping

Cover art, copyright © 2024 Alan M. Clark
Frontispiece copyright © 2024 Rebecca J. Allred
Interior illustrations copyright © 2024 by Alan M. Clark
ISBN: 979-8-9852827-7-1

Acknowledgments

Alan M. Clark would like to thank Melody Kees Clark, Lisa Snellings, Jill Bauman, Cynthia and Michael Drewek, Dave Conover, Chet Williamson, and Dianne and John Buja.

Rebecca J. Allred would like to thank Sarah Walker, Jaime Burchardt, Zach, Token, Swister, and the RFFC—you know who you are.

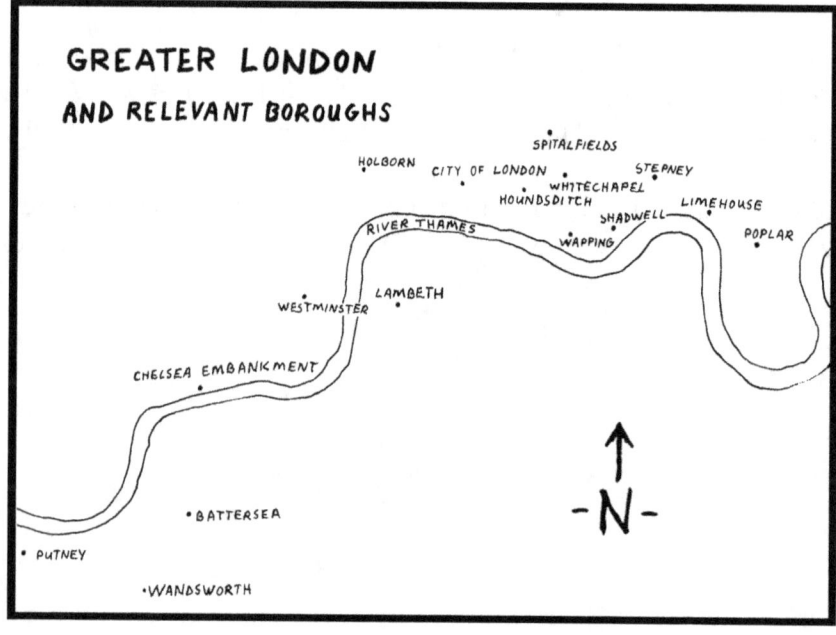

Contents

The Witch of Wapping

by Rebecca J. Allred and Alan M. Clark

IFD
Publishing

Eugene, Oregon

✀

1-The House
Wapping, London
1840

The soon-to-be occupant of the house arrives before nightfall. Through his laudanum distorted vision, he sees shadows that stretch and bend at unlikely angles in the dimming sunlight. The one he casts seems to reach eastward toward the benighted horizon, as if that one part of him might yet escape. He lingers at the edge of the footway, giving his shadow every opportunity to succeed where he, himself, has failed. One of the two women flanking him prompts him to move forward almost immediately. His silent, darkling companion gives up on escape and dutifully follows. Unperturbed, the man turns and faces what he believes will be his final destination.

The house stands two stories high and is noticeably crooked. An old neighborhood, many of the homes, especially those with overhanging upper floors, are bent or sagging. Wooden bracing between some of the houses helps keep them upright. Neighboring structures on two sides lean toward the house as if to discourage it from moving in a northwesterly direction. Dim, flickering light beckons from each of the house's three south-facing windows, one on the first floor and two above, all of them curtained to discourage curious neighbors or other, wandering eyes. The man directs his impassive gaze to the second story windows. Their curtains are as dull and gray as the eyes he's fixed upon them.

What is meant to be a place of respite and wellness is destined to become a prison and grave. And worse. The man's first inkling of what is to come occurs as his charges pull him toward the stairs running down from the right-hand side of the structure to the servants' entrance.

Gait unsteady, he descends the stairs, supported by the women to his left. Below ground level, he faces one entrance to the area and two small windows. The other woman has struck a match and lit a lamp. She turns a key in the lock and opens the door.

Before entering, as though checking to see if he has truly arrived at this moment, the man reaches up to his face, running one hand through his lion's-mane of hair, while the other tugs at his uneven beard. Both are thick and dark and wild.

Wild like him.

Wild like a rabid cur—so his nurse will say of him. She is but the first of what will seem an endless parade of women charged with feeding, bathing, and otherwise keeping the occupant of the house sedated and confined to a room on the second floor.

Wild like the rumors about the house ignited by those who pass close enough to hear the occupant's pained cries. Like a recurring fever, that gossip will burn quietly through Wapping for decades.

The laudanum has blunted his desire to turn and flee and taken all the fight out of him.

He takes a deep breath, lets it out, and enters the house.

The room on the second floor is uniquely crafted, though its contents are largely unremarkable. A bed, comfortable but not elegant, is positioned beside the north wall. A candle and a bible rest atop a small bedstead equipped with a single drawer. Inside the drawer are several fragments of charred wood and a dozen leaves of paper. Inside the Bible are a dozen more leaves of paper upon which the occupant has drawn the figures of a dozen undressed men, each in a different, provocative position.

An east-facing window peers down onto the street. The window is barred, and each of the four walls, the ceiling, and the floor are covered with a thick layer of quilted canvas padding. Even the door is insulated, except for a narrow slot at the bottom through which food and drink are passed thrice daily, and a smooth metal plate that occupies the space where a door knob and latch keyhole ought to be.

The occupant spends his time accomplishing little to nothing. Today, he worries at his teeth, which seem to him pointlessly square.

Later he sits before the door to his padded cell, lips moving imperceptibly as he utters for himself:

"I am Sir Geoffrey Webb. I am not mad.

"I am Geoffrey Webb. I am not mad, and this body is mine.

"I am Mr. Webb. I am not mad. You shall have no further say.

"I am Geoffrey. I am not mad, and I will not allow you to bite her...."

2-Rollo

Wapping, London
1897

Samuel Sutton—Sam, as we called him—saved my life when he were just eight years old. At the time, he had no cause to help me, as I were doing my wicked best to give him a nobbling.

A small kid, Sam suffered the worst of our neighborhood in Wapping. We all picked on him. He were the son of Margaret Sutton, a woman of the neighborhood that many shunned and some thought to be in league with the devil.

I don't remember how it started, but me and my mates, Zeb and Gillan, had Sam cornered in a dead end alley off Brewhouse Lane—brick and mortar and no way out. I would show everyone what a bludger I could be. I'd've been ten, a snotter guttersnipe with rampsman dreams.

"Give him a proper do-down, Rollo," Gillan shouted, and I struck Sam a blow to the bonebox.

"I don't want to fight," he said, staggering back and coming up against the bricks.

That were laughable—we *all* had to fight.

I gave Sam's smeller a blow what made it bleed.

My mates cheered.

Wiping his nose and seeing the blood come away on his hand, his face twisted into a mask so vicious, if I hadn't seen it happen, I shouldn't have recognized him. Then the bricky little squeaker flung himself at me and landed a blow to my gut, one what shouldn't have hurt as much as it did. But I'd been aching there for a few days. I fell to the wet stones, holding myself against the pain. I also held my cries to keep from embarrassing myself more than I already had done.

Gillan and Zeb, the cowards, had backed off, as if Sam, small as he were, had bested me and they'd suddenly grown afraid of him.

Sam's face lost its scowl. He looked me over with a thoughtful, troubled gaze, knelt beside me, and asked in a weary voice, "Where does it hurt?"

I tried to shrug him off and get up. A stabbing pain, what got worse as I moved, forced me to become still.

While I lay on the paving stones, he slowly pushed his stiffened fingers into the right side of my gut—uncomfortable without hurting much.

Then he pulled his fingers away quickly. That brought the pain to a sharp point, and I hashed my last meal all over us.

"Appendicitis," Sam said, wiping hash from his face. He looked to Zeb and Gillan. "Help me carry him to Mum's surgery."

They hauled me to Margaret Sutton's house in Globe Street, where she most often earned helping women end their quickening. I don't remember much about what happened until I awoke on a cot in an odd room with a stitched up hole in my gut. The drugs she'd given me before the surgery left me somewhat addled.

Margaret Sutton sat in a chair beside my cot. "I'm quite the seamstress," she said as I inspected the wound.

I'd been patched and sewn up enough in my life to know by the look of it that she had done a good job. "Thank you."

I grew uneasy with her watching me without speaking. To escape her scrutiny, I looked around.

The walls were quilted canvas, with drawings of doors and the parts of doors on the cloth. Some of the quilt stuffing hung from tears in the canvas. The true door, missing the knob on the inside, stood slightly ajar.

"Whilst you likely will not feel up to it for a while," she said, "I must ask you not to wander through the house. I am ministering to others here and I don't want you to startle them."

"What do I owe?" I asked.

"I will have to think about that," she said, "since I know you have no steady way to earn."

"Why are the walls like that?"

"Not that it's yours to know, but long ago, a member of my husband's family was kept here, an uncle named Geoffrey Webb. The man was quite mad."

A vaguely familiar name, even if I couldn't place it.

"Given the chance," she added, "he might have hurt himself or others."

Then Margaret dropped her serious tone and spoke to me almost as if to a friend. From what I knew of her, I'd say she had no friends. Her son spent more time on the street than at home. Sam did that even though he had to go up against guys like me and my mates who gave him nothing but grief. In that moment I pitied Margaret.

"Geoffrey had been knighted," she said.

"Oh, a war hero?"

"No, nothing like that," she said with a scoffing chuckle. "He was knighted for his charitable work. Otherwise, when he started causing trouble, he'd have been locked away in an asylum to rot."

"What trouble?"

"Indiscretions with young men and later some violence as well. I don't know of what sort. I think that was merely an excuse to put away a man who had become a family embarrassment. Instead of an asylum, the family put him here and kept him here for many years. In that time, he did the drawings on the walls. The padding helped keep him from hurting himself."

"Where is he now?"

"I believe he died in 1853. The house stood empty until I opened my surgery here in 1883."

Margaret stood to leave and said in her normal, too-serious voice, "Behave yourself and maybe I'll show you how they kept him from hurting his minders."

Something about her manner in that moment put a fear in me. Her slight smile had no charity or humor, as she turned away and left the room, pushing the door almost shut.

I knew I had forgot to be frightened of her. Or maybe the drugs she used on me had finally worn off and I could think again.

Everyone knew the rumors of Sam's mum being a witch. They had been around since before I came along. I imagined her returning with straps to lash me to the bed or a surgeon's knife to cut off my arms. I hadn't been so afraid since I were a small child.

And the name Geoffrey Webb stuck in my head, as if by speaking his name, Margaret had awakened the mysterious knight, himself, and he meant to pass on to me whatever madness he'd once suffered. I found myself repeating his name silently over and over. Days passed before I shook the habit.

As I healed up, Margaret checked on me now and then, often very chatty, as though she were lonely. What could she get from a conversation with the likes of me? I kept thinking she wanted something from me she didn't have the words to ask for.

The remainder of my stay, I worried what she might bring through that knobless door. Turned out, I had unfounded fears.

One day, she brought in a German game, Stern-Halma, with marbles on a board. While we played, she talked about Sam. The way she spoke of him, I didn't think she cared for him much, which left me unable to account for her next words: "Should you persuade him to come home, I'd consider your account square."

I might have been indebted to Margaret Sutton, but I owed Sam my life. If he'd decided to run away from home, I wouldn't get in his way. "He would not deem that any of my business," I told her.

Margaret Sutton looked at me, vexed. "Errands, then," she said, and stood. "Yes, my very own loblolly boy."

I didn't question her, though I knew that to be a type of ship's boy, one attached to the surgeon. She helped me to stand and showed me the door.

The debt to his mum aside, I would not forget Sam's kindness in the midst of my cruelty. Thereafter, I did my best to repay him with friendship.

3-Baby Farm
Various Boroughs of London
September 26, 1867

Young married couple seeks to adopt healthy baby.
Small premium. Write first to Mrs. M. Evans {5, Brad-
more-lane, Hammersmith.}
—*The Quotidian Advertiser*, May 15 , 1867

Miss Amelia tucked one end of a frayed white cord beneath a double loop, cinched the knot tight, and slipped the small, bound body
into a flour sack that already held another tiny infant similarly trussed
up. Those that might pass as stillbirths usually stayed out of the river,
their underdeveloped and neglected carcasses secreted away in the cof-
fins of adults like tiny stowaways to the afterlife, yet the fee for each
one, small as it was, had begun to gall her.

She couldn't fault Edgar, the undertaker. Much. Amelia understood
the value of providing an unpleasant, but necessary, service. They were,
neither of them, a charity.

While she had long since lost most of the fear that she'd be stopped
on the street and asked what she carried in her sack, she did think about
the possibility each time she hauled a load to the cemetery. Today, she
got a brief chill as she set out from her lodgings to pay Edgar a visit.

Although the Saint Mary's Cemetery in Wandsworth had exist-
ed a mere seven years, Edgar's shed, tucked into the young trees near
the Nonconformist Mortuary Chapel, had seen better days. The roof
leaked, allowing the spattering of rain outside to drip from the ceiling
inside. As Miss Amelia entered, the high autumn winds buffeted the
shed and a warm breeze passed through the structure, bearing with it
the faint odor of turned soil, rot, and mold. She held her breath until
the breeze had passed so she would not inhale the miasma it surely
carried.

Toward the back, she saw Edgar leaning over a coffin that rested upon his workbench. He waved to her and said, "Good day to you, Miss Amelia. I'll be done in a trice." He wrestled with something in the coffin, perhaps trying to remove rings from dead fingers. Approaching, she set her burden down on his bench.

Thinking again about his fee, she said, "I may have to start dumping even the smallest ones in the river myself."

Rather than haggling—or worse, taking a stab at blackmail, as she'd feared—Edgar took up the sack she'd set down, and said, "You're a good woman for taking in so many unwanted babes, but it must give you grums, watching all them little 'uns hop the twig. Ain't right." He shook his head solemnly as he nested her prior wards, little more than a pair of shrunken, wrinkled scarecrows into the coat pockets of the dead man in the coffin.

"I knows taking them babies brings in some small chink," he said. "Surely not enough to raise 'em. And when they peg out afore they're old enough to work, as so many of them do, well…"

Amelia waited patiently for him to finish. She suspected he was working himself up to bringing her in on another lurk. So far, he'd done her some good with little risk.

"…Well," Edgar repeated. Then, as if considering his words carefully, he said, "maybe I learnt a way the babies what die can help them as don't. I have a cousin, Mr. Matthew White, who works for the Credential Insurance Company…."

≥ ❋ ≤

INQUEST INTO THE DEATH OF AN INFANT

…widow, Gertrude Sutton, mother of Alice Marie Sutton, whose little body was discovered on July 1, 1867 in the Thames, gave evidence stating that on May 15, 1867 she had seen an advertisement in the paper from a person named "Evans" offering to adopt a child for the premium of £5…

…For consideration, Coroner J. Webb offered the jury an insurance document benefitting Miss Amelia Hewiston, co-signed by Matthew White.

...As part of the evidence surrounding the discovery of the body of the infant, the coroner pointed out that the knots, called a *fisherman's bend*, in the cord binding cloth to the child, were most peculiar. Since 23 other children found dead in the River Thames within the last year had been similarly bound using the same knot, the Coroner advised the jury to consider finding against Miss Hewiston.

THE VERDICT

...After the coroner summed up, the jury returned a verdict of "willful murder" against Miss Amelia Hewiston, alias Evans. Coroner Webb concluded his inquiry at the Coroner's Court into the circumstances surrounding the death of Alice Marie Sutton, 9 months.
—excerpts from the August 1, 1867 issue of *The All-Seeing Orb*

Westminster, London 1867 to 1869

Daisy Sutton, six years old and already the keeper of a terrible secret, understood the good fortune that came from Mr. and Mrs. Webb giving her Mum, Gertrude, a position in their household. Excepting that she still cried herself to sleep every night over baby Alice, Mum seemed happier than she'd ever been, and they enjoyed hot meals and having a nice warm place to sleep. More than that; Daisy saw it as the second of her secret wishes to come true. Yet despite her gratitude, she hated the coroner and his son. Just a little. *Envy is a deadly sin*, she reminded herself, but she couldn't help how she felt. She saw every kindness the elder Webb presented to her and Mum as charity, whereas the younger Webb, Stanley, who had never known fear or hunger or what it felt like to be truly cold, enjoyed kindness and good health as a matter of course. She didn't need book learning to know that wasn't fair. She couldn't help it that she didn't have a father. Nor was it her fault that she'd been born female.

Sometimes she liked to pretend the Webb's home, and all the fine things in it, belonged to her and Mum and nobody else. Stanley's tutors became Daisy's tutors and they taught her letters and maths and the Queen's English. Her daydreams ended poorly most of the time, so she didn't often encourage them. Since little truly belonged to her and she had almost no say in what and how her days went, her sweet, new life had gained a bitter edge that grew increasingly difficult to accept with each passing moon.

One night, while seated at the servants table for dinner, knowing she would not be allowed any of the spotted dick she'd helped make for the Webbs to enjoy with their dinner, she quietly whispered her newest wish aloud. She covered her mouth so none of the others, especially Mum, might read her lips. "I wish the Webb's home and all they have belonged to me."

By the time the first snow of 1869 sifted from the sky, Mum had joined baby Alice in Heaven and, once again, Daisy's secret wish had come true.

4-Rollo

Wapping, London
1898 to 1904

Turned out Sam's mum were a ream barber surgeon. That didn't mean Margaret Sutton wasn't a witch.

Back on my feet in three weeks, I introduced Sam to more of my friends. Hearing him speak, some scoffed, thinking he sounded too good for the rest of us, but he never acted that way. Once I got through with the ones what kept picking on him, most everyone let Sam be.

I were big and better at bullying than most, so my mates looked up to me. I'd been on the street since age six, when my family got evicted from our lodgings. That same year, 1893, my father, a drayman, died in an accident. His cart struck a growler and he were thrown to the paving stones. Broke his neck.

Shortly thereafter, my mum went into the Whitechapel Workhouse and never come out again—died of fever in the workhouse infirmary. I had not gone in with her because she said we would be separated. Small and slippery, I ran out of that dreary place and didn't look back, except to mourn the loss of Mum. Not long after, I took up with other kids on the street. Most of us couldn't read and write. Unwilling to work in the mills, we earned through scavenging, dipping, and hoisting.

Sam could read and write, and had some learning in medicine because of his mum. He patched us up when we got hurt, something that happened often on the River Thames, sometimes from fights with others over territory, sometimes from a simple mishap, like stepping on something sharp hidden under the water.

In payment for Margaret Sutton's surgery services, I ran errands for her until late December of 1900. Queen Margaret, I called her, as I found myself at her beck and call. She did keep me in fine fettle, tending me in illness or when I suffered a wound Sam couldn't mend. Most of what I did for her were light duty, but it went on for so long I began to steer clear of her. I avoided the neighborhood where her house stood. If I saw her out somewheres, I'd turn away and walk in the other direction.

Then she had one of her slavies deliver a threat to me that, should I not show up the next day, I'd be sorry. I didn't and I wasn't. I'd seen enough of how she used people and what she'd been willing to do to get her way. With Queen Victoria dying in January of 1901, I decided to quit the service of Queen Margaret.

One morning not long after, Sam chanced upon me where I'd been staying nights for a while: behind loose foundation stones of an abandoned building near the Wapping Old Stairs.

"Me and Mum had a row about you," he said. "She says you belong to her and I ought to make certain you know that."

I wriggled out from betwixt the foundation stones. "Ha—she wanted me to tell you the same thing. Your mum could make a stuffed bird laugh. Told her your business was none of mine, so she took me for a loblolly boy instead, only she'd not tell me when my term of service would end. It's been over a year now, Sam."

"That's her way, Rollo" he said. "Some folks never walk away for fear they might need her again in the future. She knows that and plays it for all she can get."

"Right…. Well, then I saw her demander, Dog Face Dowd, beating up little Mary Price. Mary had just come out of Redtail Becca's crib. Becca's fancyman, Alister the Onion, were paying Mary when Dog Face grabbed her. The Onion backed off. I knew I could not stand up to Dog Face, and no one else stepped in. Poor girl. I know Margaret suspected her of stealing her clients and working them on the side. Seems maybe she'd been right."

Sam nodded sadly.

I looked him right in the eye and asked, "Is that why you're here? You want me to keep doing for her?"

"No, I don't want that," he said. "Mum has turned off cruel, perhaps a bit barmy too. I've left home. For good this time. I won't go back if I can help it. What she's done to you ain't nothing to what she has Dog Face do to her willful slavies and the poor clients what can't pay."

Sam had been sounding more and more like a guttersnipe. The longer I'd known him, the better he'd got at it. "You don't have to talk like that for me," I reminded him.

He nodded, then shook his head. "It's good practice."

"Practice for what?"

"You know my father and his family will never accept me, so I need to be acceptable to my people."

"And who is that?"

"You know…"

"You mean people like me, Zeb, and Gillan."

He nodded.

"This is what that'll get you." I pointed out the opening I'd crawled from. "Smell that wet, stale air? There's little enough room and air for me inside, what with all the rats. I hope warmer weather comes before the chokedamp gets me."

I began shoving the blocks of stone back in place to hide the opening. Sam helped.

"I have something good to tell you," he said.

Finished, I brushed my hands on my kecks and turned to face him. Sam always paused before offering good news, as though that gave what he had to say more drama.

"There are twenty-one-year-old houses just abandoned in Pennington Street," he said. Again, he paused.

"Abandoned why? And what does their age matter?"

"The landlord built shoddy homes there because the land lease were for only twenty-one years. That's common for such marshy ground. Term's up. Tenants evicted. Houses in such bad shape will have to be razed, something that'll discourage any future landlord. That will take time."

"How do you know so much about it, you little squeaker?" I punched him on the shoulder and grinned.

He grinned back, giving one of his pauses.

"Come on…" I growled.

"You know that lots of women come through Mum's surgery and she had me sounding them out and seeing to their needs. While they wait, they talk, sometimes about their husbands' businesses. I listened and asked questions."

"I'd bet those houses won't be empty for long."

"Yes, that's likely. Yet most homeless won't take a chance on them.

They're too run down, maybe dangerous. Most aren't the lunatics we are." Sam gave me a big, wide-eyed smile. "The walls are only half a brick thick."

"What? They broke bricks in two?"

"No. To save materials, the wallers turned the bricks on their sides when they laid them. Should you run into one of those walls too hard, it'll crack and might fall."

"Are there squatters already?"

"Not many yet, but we'd better get to it, if we want one."

Me and Sam climbed the stairs to High Street, turned west to go around the Wapping Basin, then north toward Pennington Street.

"There's more," he said as we walked. "I met a crippled veteran who's staying in one of the houses. I brought him some food and fastened a locking latch I collected from the river onto the door to his room—it has a big, shiny black door knob."

"Will he give us trouble?"

"No. I helped him out. You know, to befriend him. I'm staying there with him now. Tired of having to fend off the squatters alone, he were glad to have me. I fancy he'd be glad to have us both and our chums too. We could defend the whole ken, Rollo. If it doesn't collapse we might see ourselves there for months."

He'd found a room for us, and a free one to boot. I had to look at Sam with fresh eyes. "You're a flash kid," I told him.

The way he smiled, I guessed that no one he looked up to, especially his mum, had ever told him he were smart before.

Near enough to the part of the river we considered our territory, we made good use of that house, me, Sam, Gillan, and Zeb. We brought in furniture salvaged from what were meant for the river—sometimes those meaning to dump old stuff into Father Thames didn't quite get the rubbish to the water. That held especially true for the big things, like furniture.

Gillan stole sailcloth from a ship in dock and we cut it up and sewed it into sacks to stuff with hay for mattresses. The way he'd talked about his fears of being caught, I doubted he'd succeed, and were surprised when he brought home the big bolt of the canvas.

The veteran, a cove named Bartholomew Bertelson—Bart, as we

called him—had been a cavalry officer, a dragoon. We helped provide for him, though he didn't do poorly at that on his own. And, as Sam had said, he were happy to have us and our mates.

That ken felt like it belonged to us, giving me the coziest feeling I'd ever had. The first few nights, we sat around drinking together and getting to know our new friend.

"I was mustered out of the service after losing my left leg in the South African War," he told us.

"Perhaps if you'd made more of an effort to find it…," I said.

He stared at me for a long moment, and I began to regret my little joke. Zeb and Gillan had worried looks, whilst Sam kept his fears— if he had any—to himself. Then a smile grew on Bart's face and he laughed so long and hard, I thought he'd suffered a spell of some sort. But he were fine, just in good humor. And the relief on my mates' faces…

"Rollo likes his humor," Sam said with a smile.

Bart were tall and dark of hair and eyes, thirty-five years old or a little older. He stood and moved about with the help of a wooden leg below the left knee. Depending perhaps on where he meant to go, he might leave the wooden leg behind and use crutches when he went out.

"How do you get on out there in London Town?" I asked him.

"My needs are few, young Rollo," he said. "By day, I beg, and bring in enough to keep myself well-corned."

Nothing if not a lushington, Bart were an easy drunk, most often in good spirits. We shared whatever we had with him, including our victuals and lush. Nights in that ken were often lost to such drunkenness that memories failed.

Bart wore his military uniform daily, washing it once every couple of weeks in a bucket he'd found at the river and patching it up if need be with a little sewing kit. He'd also kept his officer's sword and rarely went without it. In its scabbard, the blade hung beside his left hip from two leashes attached to a sword belt. "I call the sword Berty," he told us.

We had occasion to see his skills with Berty when five fellows pushed past Gillan, who had the duty to guard the door that night. Bart drew his sword, stepped forward, and blocked their way. Possibly seeing that the soldier were the only one truly dangerous, the intruders tried to overcome him. Drunk to the knockers, Bart still fought off all five of them. He'd smack them with the flat of his blade. Their leader got a welt from the hard steel on his right cheek. Two others got the same on their necks, and one took a stinging blow to his shoulder. The last, unharmed, led the retreat.

Afterward, Bart told us, "I've seen enough of war and cruelty, so I brandish Berty merely to defend and frighten. And though you saw I never once drew blood with it, those men fled because they knew they didn't stand a chance."

We saw no blood on that day, but on occasion, after returning from begging, he'd clean blood from the blade. He always had ready answers for curious looks: *I sneezed blood on the blade*, and, *I used it to clean fish for a woman at the river*, and *The dogs what follow the cat's meat man about town attacked him. I had to defend the man. Poor pups, they were just hungry,* and other such flams.

One day, as Bart left the house on crutches, Sam got curious and followed him.

"He took to the back lanes to find a public house what had set rubbish out for the rag and bone man," Sam told me later. "Finding a refuse bin brimming with cast-offs—half-decent pig wash should you ask me—he also found rats. They scurried to get away. Quick with Berty, he skewered one. Even wounded, it almost got away. He stepped on it to put it out of its misery, then pulled from his pocket a length of white cloth, and smeared blood from the rat onto it. Bart wound that like a bandage over his leg stump, making it look like a fresh wound."

I chuckled to hear it. "He *is* a clever bastard," I said.

Sam nodded.

"Bart took a spot at a crossing near Tower Bridge. He used a piece of chalk to write on the footway, 'Veteran of the Boer War. Don't allow those who fought for Queen and country to go hungry.' He set beside that a box to receive donations."

"I won't let him go hungry," I told Sam. "He's the reason we don't have more competition in Pennington Street."

"Well," Sam said, "Bart saw me trying to stay hidden, as I ducked behind folks using the footway. He motioned for me to join him.

"'Now that you've seen how I got so rich,' he says around a grin, 'don't think I see you boys as beneath me.'"

I laughed. 'No,' I tells him, 'but I'll keep it from the others if you wish.'

"'No need for that,' says he. 'Now, go away and let me do what I must.'"

We shared that drafty house for five years. The worst of it came in winter. The roof had five big leaks and many piddling ones. The rain and weather came right in. Plenty of rot and mold. Still, it were better lodgings than most of what I'd known.

Over time, Margaret Sutton must have come to understand that Sam had truly left her. As she'd tried with me, she sent several of her indentured servants to persuade Sam to return to her. Some laid threats, some offered reward to him should he return, none succeeded.

On a day in August of 1902, Bart donned his uniform, took up his crutches, and left the house and didn't return for three days. We worried something had happened to him, and had decided to look for him just about the time he returned home, looking wrung out.

"I went to join my brothers," he says, "lining the route of the procession for the coronation of King Edward. Then I got drunk with Axel Batts, who I fought beside in South Africa. We went to his home. His wife, Ophelia, fed me, if reluctantly. Though she made it plain that she wanted to be rid of me, I stayed and drank with Axel for two days and nights. I'd do it again tomorrow, given an excuse."

Dog Face Dowd come to the house in Pennington Street at dusk one cold day in December of 1903. He knocked on the door and, as luck would have it, Sam answered, not knowing who he'd be receiving.

Dowd grabbed Sam by the collar and hauled him out onto the footway. "Your mum wants you, and I'm here to make certain you heed her wishes."

I followed them outside into the growing dark. Dowd turned to me, said, "Rollo, you're next." His breath puffed out white in the cold air.

Margaret Sutton didn't have an indenture contract with me, and I almost said as much, but I knew better than to challenge him. The truth would not have persuaded Dowd.

Like a school marm, Dog Face held Sam by the left ear and marched him off down the lane, I guessed toward Globe Street and his mum.

Me and Zeb followed. As usual, when there might be a fight, Gillan couldn't be found.

At a crossing, Bart come up from our left. "Unhand that boy."

Dog Face bore down on Sam's ear and twisted. Sam screamed.

"He's going home to his mum," Dowd said.

A couple across the lane turned and fled. Other's farther away lingered to watch the goings-on.

"I don't think his mum wants you to harm him," Bart said.

Dowd let go of Sam, crouched, and reached for something in the side of his boot. Standing up, he held out an eight-inch-long knife and waved it in the air.

In the gloom, I don't think he'd seen that Bart had a sword. As the demander heard the long, cold steel sliding out of its scabbard, his eyes got wide.

Bart smiled. "Do you want me to wait here while you go get a longer blade?"

Dowd seemed to get a look at the wooden leg Bart wore. "Do you want me to wait here while you go find your other leg?"

Bart laughed. "Almost as funny as another joke I heard about my leg." He winked at me.

At that, any small fears I had for the soldier became smaller still.

Dowd moved in a slight crouch toward Bart, holding his blade in his right hand. He should have been afraid, but, then, he didn't know what we knew about Bart and his Berty.

Windows, shutters, and doors opened in the houses facing the street. Like crows hoping for carrion, curious onlookers hung out of the windows to watch the fray.

Big as he was, Dowd moved fast. He slipped to his right, perhaps to gain the advantage of fighting on Bart's weaker side. The soldier smacked the demander on the right forearm with the flat of his blade. The sting of that must have forced Dowd to drop the knife. The weapon hit the cobblestones with a ringing sound. Dowd grabbed his right arm and backed away. Working his right hand and soothing the muscles of the forearm with his left, a look of fear took hold of him for a moment what passed so quickly, I'd have missed it had I glanced away.

Then Dowd charged. Untroubled, Bart turned easily on his wooden leg, and the demander fell past him. The soldier put the point of his sword through the ankle of Dowd's left boot. The cove screamed, defeated, and fell to the paving stones, rolling and holding his bloody foot.

"You will rue this day," Dog Face growled. "I'll see you dead."

Bart gestured for us to head back the way we'd come.

"He's a very bad cove," Sam whispered. "He's family people."

"He *will* come after you," I told the soldier.

"Rollo," Bart said, "he's a mad dog what needed putting down. Short of killing him, I did just that. I severed his Achilles tendon. Even Sam's mum couldn't fix that. He's not going anywhere without help."

The show over, onlookers closed their doors and windows and returned to whatever they'd been doing before the disturbance. People moved along the lane again. As we walked back toward the house, Dog Face Dowd's curses and moans dwindled to silence in the distance.

A month later, in January of 1904, our house fell in. Bart were the only one inside.

By the time enough tile, brick, mortar, and beam had been cleared away to get to the soldier, he had, as we say, laid down the knife and fork. We found his sword, bent in two places, under a broken beam.

Although none of us believed his death an accident, we had nothing to prove our suspicions. A constable, who had been talking to our neighbors in Pennington Street, caught us at the river and threatened to keep an eye on us if we didn't help with the investigation. Since Bart had got into trouble defending one of us, we decided we owed it to him to do something and gave evidence at the inquest. Weren't a difficult thing. Of course, we knew nothing but that Dog Face had made a threat. Fearing his family, we kept quiet about that while telling ourselves Bart had indeed put the demander down. After all, Dog Face now hobbled around with a large, stiff boot on his bad foot, so fewer feared him man to man.

Bart were buried in a ten-foot-deep pauper's grave in Stepney along with six other poor souls. Me and my mates attended. As we waited for the vicar, Gillan kept bemoaning the dreadful stench. I glared at him and finally he shut his bonebox.

Only one other did we meet there besides the vicar, a woman who introduced herself as Penelope Bertelson. "I am Bart's wife," she said.

"Did he perhaps say why he didn't return to me after the war?"

None of us had an answer for her. I had a notion I couldn't bring myself to share.

"We knew him from the street, " Sam said. "A beggar, he were."

She got a pained look, and I gave Sam the eye for speaking in such an unvarnished manner.

"He sent his pension to me every month through a postal order," Penelope said. "If you young men had not given evidence at the inquest, I might never have found him. Thank you."

"The least we could do for a friend, ma'am," I said.

"A fine fellow," Gillan mumbled.

"He could out-drink me any day," Zeb said, "and my mate's will tell you, that takes some doing."

She listened politely, whilst we spoke of the things we wanted to recall of Bart. Zeb stared at her, looking like a lost pup. Though too old for him, I think he were quite smitten with Penelope. She had a true beauty to her. I fancy all of us tried to picture her with Bart. As pretty as all that, she could have had anyone, which only made Bart seem larger still.

"You have my condolences," Sam said.

Sad watching her walk alone from that small field what reeked of rotting corpses. The late sun cast her long shadow, nearly as black as her mourning clothes, onto the green behind her.

Sam, indeed a quick-witted fellow, discovered another condemned house for us to fetch up in. The abode sat across a thin lane from the Shadwell rail station. Not as old as the last house and more sturdy, it still shook every time a train came through the station, and the coal soot set us all to coughing.

One night as we sat drinking, Gillan said, "This black will be our death." He showed what he'd coughed into his hand. Black specks appeared amidst his white spittle foam.

"What, you want to live forever?" I asked. He would complain if offered a purse of gold sovereigns, I decided.

Gillan looked at the floor, Zeb shrugged, and Sam shook his head. A moment later, he asked, "Rollo, do you think Mum had Bart killed?"

Not that any of us didn't think so, but no one had suggested it until then. "I don't know," I told him. "Might have been his family."

✣
5-Stanley
Westminster, London
1870

Something he couldn't pin down about the little Sutton girl both vexed and intrigued Stanley Webb. Perhaps it had something to do with her silence. She'd always been quiet, but never in the same way as other servants. *She holds her tongue in secrecy,* he decided. *What is she hiding?*

Something in her manner also troubled him. Though Daisy fulfilled her duties helping her mum with chores—turning down the beds, lighting fires, and helping prepare meals—she might easily have been mistaken for a member of the family. She was the only girl, other than his mother, who looked Stanley and his father right in the eyes. Even when scolded, Daisy never dropped her gaze.

She grew only more bold in the months following her mum's death and Father's decision that Daisy would stay. Not a sister, but near enough now that Stanley would earn a scolding should he choose to torment the girl too eagerly.

But the way she looked at him! Her eyes at the same time hard and probing, yet wary. As if Daisy knew something Stanley didn't know—*couldn't* know. As if she compared him to a rat and found the rodent more worthy. Worthy of what, he couldn't begin to guess. Unaccustomed to that sort of judgment and scrutiny, Stanley began doubting himself for the first time in his life.

To make matters worse, Daisy had also shown a talent for learning, a trait Stanley believed had much to do with his father's decision to informally adopt the girl.

Once, following a rather dreary performance in maths on Stanley's part, Father had remarked, "Perhaps I should send Daisy to university in your stead."

An absurd threat to be sure, but it hadn't felt absurd in the moment, and the next time his father asked Stanley about his maths, the boy had nothing but good news to report. Still, a part of him feared Daisy might come up with a way to replace him. Stanley kept his eyes and ears open for any chance to throw her to the wolves.

In the evenings until called for bed, Daisy often excused herself after supper, slipping back into less formal, possibly for her more comfortable surroundings: the root cellar, down in the area. Stanley firmly believed she got up to more than enjoying the peace and quiet down there, but his parents dashed every effort on his part to discover her true activities. Father had said it might take some time for Daisy to feel at home, and instructed Stanley and his mother to do the girl a courtesy and ignore any odd behavior, so long as she wasn't harming anything or anyone.

Stanley's chance came one evening when Mother and Father entertained guests. While the adults gossiped and smoked, Stanley lit a lamp and crept down to the area and into the root cellar to spy on Daisy.

As he descended the stairs, he doused his light. A lit candle lamp stood on a shelf just inside the root cellar to his right. Standing silently and looking in through the door, he didn't see her. At first he thought she'd found a way to sneak out. Entering and crouching down out of the light, he saw that the girl had merely flattened herself against the dirt floor in a way that made her easy to overlook. Belly pressed to the packed clay and muttering quietly, Daisy took a crust of bread from her left hand and placed it under a shelf of preserves.

"Caught you!" Stanley shouted, springing to his feet.

Daisy also gained her feet and spun to face her accuser. For once, she looked like the urchin she truly was, frightened, small, and dirty. Stanley stood as tall and menacing as he could, like an executioner glowering down from atop the gallows stairs.

"Daisy Sutton, just you wait until my father learns you've been stealing food."

A relaxed calm replaced it so quickly, Stanley wasn't sure if the confusion that briefly clouded her eyes had been real or if he'd imagined it. And because Daisy confessed immediately, he didn't have occasion to consider it until later.

"Yes," she said, almost eagerly. "That's what I'm doing."

"You will wait there until Father comes to see."

They stayed that way until his parents' guests had gone, Stanley looming over Daisy to preserve the evidence, Daisy waiting patiently, almost as if she'd foreseen the encounter. When at last his mother called for them to come to bed, Stanley shouted, "Father, come and see the crime I've uncovered."

Daisy stood, maddeningly without an expression, even as Father arrived.

"She's a thief," Stanley said, as though confirming a long suspected rumor. "Been nicking extra bread after supper."

Stanley crossed the floor to Daisy, snatched her fisted left hand and pulled it forward into the dim light. She opened her fingers to reveal mangled bread crust inside.

Daisy didn't flinch or cry. She didn't deny the accusation or make excuses or apologize. That she showed no fear vexed Stanley the most. She stood, waiting patiently for his father to pass judgment as though she had nothing to lose, as if being exposed as a liar and a thief was no more scandalous than receiving poor marks in school.

"Stanley."

"Sir?" Stanley braced himself for the praise certain to follow.

"Your mother is calling you for bed."

"Daisy's not in trouble?" Stanley asked, dumbfounded and disappointed.

"Tell your mother I'll bring Daisy up shortly."

"But—"

"Good night, Stanley."

His father stepped aside, gesturing for Stanley to exit the cellar and denying him the satisfaction of witnessing any drama that might follow. *An unbearable injustice*, he thought. But Stanley knew better than to argue with his father, so he let go of Daisy's hand and did his best to conceal the bitterness festering inside him as he retreated to their shared bedroom.

After speaking to his mother, Stanley lay on the bed in the half-dark, straining his ears for any hint of Father's raised voice or Daisy's high, warbling cry. The thought of her wrongdoing going unpunished seemed absurd. Nevertheless, Mother had just doused the lights when Daisy's silhouette appeared in the open doorway without so much as a sniffle to signal her upset. In the dark, Stanley silently turned his back to her. She slipped inside quietly. He heard the soft shuffle of feet crossing the floorboards and the creak of the bed's wooden joints as she settled the weight of her small body onto the edge of his mattress. Too angry to play any of her dumb bedtime games, Stanley would ignore the Sutton girl until she grew bored and went to her own bed.

"I'm sorry, I lied," she said.

For a moment, he thought Father must have scolded her after all and instructed Daisy to apologize. If he feigned sleep, he could tell Father that she hadn't yet rendered the apology when asked the following morning. He could force her to do it all again, and in front of everyone. With the exception of his deep, too-steady breathing, Stanley held himself very still.

"But I couldn't let him find her," Daisy continued, as though she knew he could hear her. "She was hungry and needed help, so I gave her my scraps, you know, like pig wash for the servants. But then Mr. Webb says—" She paused, lowering her voice even more and leaning in close. "I mean, *Father* says, should I want more food, all I need do is ask."

Stanley barely succeeded in holding himself down and remaining quiet as the upstart planted a dry kiss on his cheek.

"Thank you," she said. "I know you didn't mean to help, but you did me a good turn."

Unable to stand her bumptiousness any longer, Stanley sat up. He would have spit when the Sutton girl declared joint-possession of his father, had his tongue not shriveled like a dead leaf in the sun and his mouth dried to dust. Stanley wanted to cry out! Push her away! Beg his mother and father to send her to an orphanage where she belonged! Right now! Tonight!

She responded as if he'd spoken his thoughts and desires aloud. "Mind yourself, Stanley Webb," she whispered. And while Daisy's sweet voice had a tinge of concern, Stanley recognized a warning when he heard one.

Moonlight puddled in the windowsills, illuminating the room enough for Stanley to see her eyes and that she wasn't joking. His eyes asked what his trembling lips and throat could not.

"Or I might make *you* gone, too. I didn't mean for baby Alice to die, but I did wish for her to be gone so Mum and I could live somewhere warm, with food enough to fill our bellies. When I wished for this to be my house so I'd never have to leave, I didn't mean for Mum to die either."

Something like a confession, her story of fulfilled wishes also reinforced the promise of a threat. Daisy held Stanley's gaze.

"Even though I didn't mean for them to die, I guess that's the price for having my wishes come true. Should you be cruel to me, Stanley, I might make another wish." She stood and crossed the room to her own bed. Daisy pulled back the top bedclothes, and, as she nestled into them, said, "I might even miss you a little sometimes, same as I miss Alice and Mum."

In the silence that followed, Stanley marked the passage of time counting each thud of his walloping heart. Once he'd grown calmer, he crept out of the bedroom, lit a lamp, and carried it down into the root cellar. He set the lamp on the dirt floor near the place he'd spied Daisy less than an hour earlier. Once on his hands and knees, Stanley found he still couldn't see under the bottommost shelf. He got all the way down on his belly as Daisy had done while, he now presumed, trying to feed something.

Stanley lowered himself into the dirt and pressed his cheek to the cold, hard-packed ground. This time of year the root cellar should smell faintly and pleasantly of onions and stale potatoes. Instead, Stanley could not escape the night air wafting from the brick-walled cesspit that yawned on the other side of the room, just below the indoor privy. Father hadn't had it emptied in a long while.

Stanley held his breath and pushed the lamp closer to the shelves and the something beneath that recoiled from its flickering light.

6-The House
Wapping, London
1853

To his horror, Sir Geoffrey Alton Webb did bite his first nurse. That seemed to be more than she'd bargained for. She quit her employment with the Webb family, and they swiftly replaced her.

Since arriving in the room, Geoffrey had spent more than a little time concentrating on how to get through the door that had no knob. He willed it to open, and when that didn't work, he set about to create through art the mechanism it lacked: a latch with doorknob. Hard to draw on the blank latch plate, he instead drew on the quilted wall nearby with charcoal, then tried to lift the knob he'd drawn from its two dimensional situation. He could not get his hands around it.

His first night in the room, he dreamed that the door lay above him, trapping him in a dark hole under water. Plenty of fresh air just beyond the threshold would be his should he find the doorknob and get it open.

He woke up gasping for air, and crying out for help. No one came, but at least the sensation of drowning had ceased with wakefulness.

Geoffrey decided that the knob he had drawn wasn't rendered well enough, that it lacked the quality of being substantial. He practiced, drawing it over and over in different parts of the room, striving to make it look and feel more substantial. He would believe he'd captured the right look, only to find that he still could not wrap his fingers around the knob. One attempt frustrated him so much that he tore the section of canvas he'd drawn on from the wall. He carried that to the door and tried to somehow fasten it to the blank latch plate. When that didn't work, he tried drawing it on paper and fastening that to the latch plate. Failing again, he decided he didn't understand doors well enough, and began to practice drawing them, along with latches, knobs, and hinges.

Nearly every night he felt the door pressing down on him in a watery dream, and would awaken choking and gasping. Each time, he had felt all along the edges of the door, trying to find its knob, and having no luck.

Geoffrey got the idea that if he drew a different door and he did it well enough to make it physically tangible, the original door in the wall might go away, hopefully also removing the threat it posed in dreams. Then he might use the new door to escape.

Nothing worked. His efforts and the thoughts behind them ran like a musical fugue through his head, the winding repetition of themes growing more and more maddening.

Years passed while he kept trying, and got little sleep.

Unable to control the urge that seemed to come from someone inside him, he bit twelve more nurses. Number four, the first to be offered any protecting garments, had been given heavy leather gloves. With each subsequent bite, and the location of that bite considered, the leather shielding offered to Geoffrey's nurses grew—from the leather gloves to gauntlets to sleeves, from a leather apron to a leather bodice and leggings, from a simple leather mask to a flexible helmet for full head protection—until it had become a full-body affair, the sight of which, in itself, discouraged many potential employees from taking the position.

The thirteenth nurse, Angelina Dubois, now lies at the foot of the stairs in a pool of her own blood. She grips her neck in a feeble effort to staunch the flow from the soft tissue where, moments earlier, the madman had buried his teeth. She hasn't the time to regret not tucking the hem of the helmet into the collar of the leather bodice. Trying unsuccessfully to rise, she sees the front door is flung wide. She knows that, along with her ward, she has lost her position, and possibly her life....

Nothing about what Geoffrey did on that day gives explanation to the mystery of how he escaped.

7-Samuel and the Stranger
Wapping, London
1905

"I bite you!"

The woman's gleeful voice came the moment I felt a searing pain in my left ankle.

I'd stepped into a well of mud in the Thames foreshore that took my left shoe—sucked it right off my foot. Upon my next stumbling step, I heard a crunch and the voice, felt the pain. I took a tumble onto the mud and gravel.

My chums gathered round. Laughing, they stood over me.

"Sam, he's arfarfan'arf!" Zeb shouted.

"Take care he don't throw an arf on you," Gillan said.

Plenty drunk, we were, and my friends would not miss a chance to mock me as I'd have done to any of them, should the boot be on the other foot.

Lying where I'd fallen, I looked around for the owner of the female voice, saw naught but my friends, the foreshore, and the Thames, cocooned within the light morning fog.

"Here's your shoe, Sam," Gillan said, offering me what looked like a great glob of raw clay. "Oi, you're bleeding!"

"You don't hear *him* crying about it," Rollo scoffed.

Whilst Gillan and Zeb had some fear of Rollo, he'd become my champion among those of the street, always persuading others that I was a ream fellow, despite being educated.

Rollo moved to help me up. As soon as I put weight on the naked foot, I cried out and dropped my fouled left shoe.

"There're teeth where you stepped," Zeb said. "That must be your blood on them. They don't look like animal teeth."

Rollo and Zeb lifted and carried me. A trail of blood marked our course across the foreshore, up the causeway, and the Union Stairs.

Somewhere in the passage that led to High Street, as my chums jostled me past the usual noisy covey of smoking pinchcocks, I became insensible.

I awoke at the house in Globe Street, Wapping where I'd spent much of my youth and where my Mum, Margaret Sutton, still lived and practiced her illegal trade. I lay in the cot in my old bedroom, the padded cell where my mad great-uncle Geoffrey had been held for years. Mum sat beside me in a chair, dressing my wound.

My chums had got me as far as her doorstep before abandoning me, helpless as a newborn. They'd not admit it, but I knew Zeb and Gillan actually believed some of the stories whispered about Mum, and while she wasn't a witch, there were plenty of reasons not to like the woman sitting beside me. That wasn't the first time they'd done a dump and scoot at Mum's. They had done the same to Rollo years earlier when he'd had appendicitis. On that day, I'd remained to tell Mum about Rollo and help her get him into my old bedroom. I didn't fault my chums for wanting naught to do with her.

As soon as she noticed me blinking and gawking at the room, Mum bore down on the gash in my left ankle. She squeezed her eyelids nearly shut to make mean, little slits of her gaze, as if she might make me smaller by sight alone.

This was not the first time Mum had ministered to my ailments. She'd always been unhappy to do so. I knew that anything I might say or do would goad her to further unhappiness or anger, so I kept a sober face and my mouth shut.

"Your pals dropped you on the footway, rang the bell, and fled. The cowards. What are they afraid of? Me?"

When I gave no reply, she bore upon the wound again until I cried out. Blood welled up around her thumb where it pressed against the white dressing.

First do no harm didn't apply to ne'er-do-well sons. Had I voiced the complaint aloud, she might have told me that she wasn't recognized by the Royal College of Surgeons because of her gender. Her husband, Stanley, had helped her buy a medical degree from a university in Scotland, and that sufficed as long as she and her medical practice weren't scrutinized.

"I would offer something for the pain, but you are already the worse for drink. Now, what troubles do you bring to my door?"

"I were harmed nearby—" I began.

"I *was* harmed nearby," she corrected. She didn't like me sounding like the street, a habit she'd worked hard to rid herself of and one I'd got into in an effort to better fit in.

"My friends brought me here because they believed you could help," I told her, "and that you'd not leave your son to suffer on the street. I'll leave as soon as I'm able."

She frowned, pointing at the long gashes in my heel and ankle. "Did you get that at the river?"

"Yes," I said, "at the river." No reason to be dishonest. She knew about our mudlarking.

"You were wearing only one shoe?"

I didn't choose to explain.

The look on her face wasn't fit for family or foe, although in her eyes, I might've been both. She hadn't been glad to see me for a couple of years. Mum had once been married to a proper physician, Stanley Webb. He'd turned her out in the street shortly after my birth. They finally divorced the year I turned eleven. Margaret said father had found himself a more suitable wife and that had been the last she'd said of him.

Though it cost her marriage and station, Margaret Webb, Miss Sutton following the divorce, raised me on her own. She was anything but a loving mother, and at age twelve, I left home to find my own way.

"I pulled this from the wound. You'll be lucky if you don't get an infection." Mum flicked whatever had lodged itself in my foot onto the bed. She took up her needle and thread, the bandage roll, and the scissors, put them in her medical kit, and left the room, shutting the door behind her. Since I'd stolen from her on occasion—well, often enough—she would only have me so long as she might keep me locked away from the rest of her home. The door to my room had no knob on the inside, just a flat metal plate to cover where one must have once been. I heard Mum turning a key in the lock from the outside.

The room's soft walls and padded floor had dampened the sound of mad Uncle Geoffrey's indecipherable ravings, allowing his keeper to use the other rooms and preventing all but those passing nearest to the house from hearing him. The few that did hear, whispered about the strange sounds, and the house gained a reputation for being haunted, among other things.

Uncle Geoffrey had drawn doors, doorknobs, Keys, and keyholes on the canvas walls. Like everyone who came to the house on Globe Street, I think he looked for a way out.

The last of his caretakers, a large woman in her middle years, died while carrying out her duties and her corpse lay undiscovered for over a week. Since he had no way to get out of the room and no one came to check on him, Geoffrey Webb might have perished from lack of water. Yet, in some manner unknown to his keepers, he escaped.

All that had been long before I came along. That hadn't always been my room. I'd once had a chamber on the ground floor. Growing up, I'd been plagued with bad dreams. The kind that make a kid wake up screaming, even if he can't remember much about them. Sharp teeth snapping at me. That's it. Even with much more happening in the dreams, that's all I could remember. Got so the nightmares happened often enough, Mum moved me into the padded cell on the second floor so I'd disturb her clients less. Over four decades after Uncle Geoffrey had died, the padded walls did a fair job muffling my nightmare screams. Even so, the few who got close enough to the house in the night might well have heard me, keeping alive the rumor that the house was haunted and thus Mum a witch.

One night, the dreams got so bad and my screams so wild, Mum finally came to unlock the door and check on me. I knocked her down as I burst out and fled down the stairs and away into the night.

Afraid of what Mum would do when I returned home, I spent the next three days and nights fighting, hiding, and sleeping on the streets of Wapping. Though cold and hungry, the sharp teeth let me be and I didn't once wake up screaming. That remained true every time I ran away. The only nights I slept soundly were those I spent away from home. Bad dreams combined with Mum's constant criticism—no wonder I felt more at home on the street.

The object Mum dug from my left ankle was a thin grey splinter, shiny on one side. Trying to guess what it had come from, it crossed my mind that perhaps it came from the wood of Zeb's magical foreshore door. A bitter smile touched my lips.

Zeb had been leading us to a door latch he'd discovered poking up out of the gravel of the foreshore. "I think it's the latch you put on Bart's door," he said, "the one with the shiny black doorknob. Those what hauled our old house away must have dumped it all in the river."

Bart, now dead, had been a good friend, a soldier we shared a house with.

"We might want it for remembrance of Bart," Zeb said. "If not, it'd be worth something at the marine store. I couldn't get it to come up. Must still be attached to the door and its frame, resting just under the surface."

He looked to Rollo. "Should you succeed in picking the lock—"

"I can pick *any* lock," Rollo said.

"Well, yes," Zeb said. He looked away, unable to meet the bigger boy's terrible gaze. "Then we could pry open the door and get it loose from the inside."

"Unlock a *door* in the fore*shore*?" Rollo sang, trying to mock Zeb's tone. Not intended, he made it sound magical.

"Yes," Zeb said, "so we can get the latch off. It's bolted on from the other side."

When we got to the spot where he'd found the door latch, it rested atop the mud, not attached to anything.

"I thought—" Zeb began.

"You *thought*…" Rollo said. "That's doubtful."

I had the largest pockets, so they'd given the thing to me to carry.

With my injury on that day, all had forgot about the door latch and knob. The thing still bulged from a pocket of my jacket, which, along with my right shoe, lay upon the seat of the chair Mum had used. My mud-caked left shoe might have remained on the foreshore, where I'd dropped it.

An uneven tapping at the window got me to sit up. I tried for the chair, barely able to reach it, although it stood beside the door, just a couple of feet away. Pulling it close to the bed, I almost tipped it over. My jacket and shoe fell to the floor. I slid onto the chair, and used my good foot to push myself over to the window. I lifted the curtain and looked out between the iron bars that had been installed long ago to keep Uncle Geoffrey in.

Zeb stood below the window on the footway outside. When he saw me, he waited until those walking nearest to him had passed by, then opened his jacket to show what he had half hidden inside. A human skull rested in the crook of his arm, its lower jaw missing. He held the skull upside down, and I could see that its upper jaw had been crushed. The inside of the skull held mud and gravel. He quickly covered it as others moving along the footway drew near to him.

"I found it under the foreshore," he said loud enough for me to hear through the window pane. "I dug it out of the gravel. That's what you stepped on." He gestured to the upper jaw. "The teeth must have done you. I bet it belonged to one of the pirates hanged at the Execution Dock over a hundred years ago or more."

I nodded, though I doubted the skull belonged to a pirate. The Execution Dock had stood out over the river from Wapping because the Admiralty, who ruled on the seas for the Queen, had no legal power on land. Rotted away long ago, no one knew exactly where the dock had stood. And since those hanged were either carted off to be buried in unmarked graves or given to the medical men to be anatomized, why would they have left a head behind?

"I thought you would like to see it before I take it to the River Police," Zeb said. "Should they offer reward, I'll share it with you."

Again, I nodded, yet I didn't think the mutton shunters would reward him.

Zeb turned and walked down the lane toward High Street and turned easterly.

My damaged foot, swollen and hot, fairly throbbed, blood pulsing through it as Zeb's words brought back memory of the woman's voice. *I bite you!*

Thoughts of what Mum had pulled from my foot and Zeb's suggestion that it had come from a skull that had belonged to a long dead pirate, threatened to tip me out of the chair and onto the floor. My gut roiled, and my head swam as if I were drowning in my own blood. I felt like I'd returned to childhood and my nightmares had come true. *What poison got inside me off those teeth?*

I returned to lie in the cot with what I now believed to be a splinter of tooth clutched tightly in one hand. A bit fearful that the unknowable dreams of my youth might return, I sought sleep with little success at first. The cot had a thin straw mattress, and a pillow and quilt that smelled of sickness and strangers. The slumber I did find held not the nightmares of my childhood, but the dreams of yet another wounded person, a woman I did not know.

Curious dreams of late. Though piecemeal, they run, one into another, like they belong to a whole. And I cannot remember rising during the days what must come between. Knapped and sleeping rough in Battersea Park, I have slept but fitfully for a long while. With the need for rest, perhaps I've slept through a day or more. Truly, I can't say I am awake, even now as I try to recall.

Somehow, I am not whole. I see little through cloth stretched over my eyes like a shroud. Whilst I should be troubled to find myself in such a state, I cannot put my thoughts together well enough to make sense of it or to do anything about it.

I feel my left leg at some distance, bobbing in water whilst the rest of me feels little. My undergarments are sodden, plastered to my chilled flesh. The sounds of children bathing or playing in the water come to me.

Also at some remove, I feel my belly swelling uncomfortably. And it comes to me that the surgeon has done as I asked. The infant has been flushed or rinsed away. Yet to get it done, I have been emptied out. Would be more frightening if I felt pain. There is none. And all the fears what came with being alone, knapped, and destitute are gone. I am glad to be rid of the child.

The cloth over my eyes falls away and I see that I am in murky water. Alarmed, I want to wave my arms and legs about, as I've seen swimmers do. Nothing comes of my desire. Still, my head rises close enough to the surface that I can see children's hands grasping my leg and lifting it from the water. I must believe that, should I be patient, they will pull all of me to shore.

A soft breeze cools the skin of my thigh. Curious that I am not ashamed to be touched.

✄
8-Fragments from the Press
1853-1870

Suicide or Hoax?

Numerous sightings of Sir Geoffrey Alton Webb were reported last evening by concerned and well-meaning bystanders, including quite respectable persons, some of whom had known him before his disappearance. The gentleman in question, once knighted by the Queen for his philanthropic efforts on behalf of the poor, has been missing since 1840. Although the person sighted wore little but rags and had a wild, anguished look about him, those questioned said that the figure they saw run out onto London Bridge and throw himself into the Thames was indeed Sir Geoffrey Alton Webb. A rescue attempt yielded no sign of the gentleman. The Police are actively investigating the matter.

—the morning edition of *The Illuminating Star*, July 22, 1853

The Bitings Continue

More on the biting assaults that have plagued the City of London and particularly the districts of Wapping and Shadwell since July 30, 1853. On that date in Billingsgate Fish Market, an unknown assailant attacked and bit a young man of 16 years on the shoulder. He succumbed to infection of the wound. Since the majority of the attacks have occurred in Shadwell, the press has dubbed the perpetrator of these crimes The Shadwell Shark. Within the last 9 years, 22 men, 16 women, and 11 children under the age of 14 have also been bitten, three of the bites so deep and severe the victims spent time in hospital recovering. The latest incident occurred this Friday past in Whitechapel Road. The victim, Jushia Boynton, a man of 20 years, rushed to the aid of a friend about to be bitten. The assailant turned on Boynton and succeeded in taking a bite out of his right palm before running away. "I believe he swallowed that part of me," Boynton said. He described the assailant as an elderly, hooded tatterdemalion with jagged, if not sharpened teeth. His description of the man matches those given by some of the other victims. He was treated at the London Hospital and is expected to recover. The police are again asking the public for help with information or sightings of the assailant.

—*The All-Seeing Orb,* May 17, 1862

A Tosher's find

Alfred Coogery, a tosher, discovered in the sewers a deceased man bearing a remarkable resemblance to Sir Geoffrey Alton Webb, who has been missing since 1840, but who may have been seen leaping from London Bridge in July of 1853. For a variety of reasons, including the advanced age of the body at the time of death, the police cannot say for certain that the corpse is truly that of the celebrated philanthropist, Webb.

—*The Signal,* November 16, 1870

9-Inquest into a Death from Overlaying, Coroner J. Webb Presiding
Wandsworth, London
1869

Coroner John Webb asked the witness, Mary Ann Wigden, a few questions to confirm what his initial inquiries had told him about the case: the identity of the deceased and the location and time the death occurred. Once satisfied, he looked to the Jury Foreman, Mr. Phelps, who stood by trying to look important and failing.

Mr. Phelps nodded, glanced at a note in his hand, and turned to Mrs. Wigden. "The jury would like you to explain what you mean when you say that the death of your child, Sarah Stahl Wigden, in your bed is no one's fault."

"A good wife and mother, I am," Mrs. Wigden said, looking small and helpless. She took rapid breaths and held her forehead in one hand, while the other, white-knuckled, gripped the dark wood rail of the witness box.

"Take your time, madam," Coroner Webb said. Struggling to find a more comfortable position for his aching back, he reminded himself to practice forbearance.

Mrs. Wigden looked to him as she began to speak with some hesitation. "Well, sir, too many of us—uh—in one kife. Simple as that."

"By kife, you mean bed?"

"Yes, sir. I apologize, sir."

"No need," he said. "I have some knowledge of every-day terms."

"Sir, to understand what happened, you have to know how we live and work, and how little we have." She lowered her gaze and her mouth became a hard, thin line.

"You are not on trial," Coroner Webb said, "and you are not the only one to have lost an innocent child in this remarkably sad manner. Indeed, the numbers of the city's infants perishing in this way have been increasing year after year, nearly five hundred over-laying cases within the last twelve months. We want to better understand how this happens."

At thirty-five years of age, Mrs. Wigden looked to be fifty years old. Coroner Webb saw that her eyes shed proper tears, not the sort he so often saw from the guilty. Yet some of the jury, including the foreman, had looks of skepticism that no doubt frightened the poor woman.

"Don't be afraid," the coroner said. "Just tell us in your own words what happened."

"Well, sir," she began, "whenever my husband, Gordon, asks, I gives it," Embarrassment gripped her features and, again, she lowered her gaze.

"That's quite enough of *that*, madam," the foreman said amidst muttering from the jury.

"No," Coroner Webb said, "Please, Mrs. Wigden, do continue."

The foreman shook his head to register his disgust.

"So young, I were, when we wed," Mrs. Wigden said, "I didn't know any better. I didn't know about the ways to keep from getting knapped, and now we have twelve children."

"Have some respect for Coroner Webb, and these proceedings," the foreman chided.

"That's all right, Mr. Phelps," the coroner said. "I wish to hear what she has to say, however she wishes to say it."

The foreman had a look of impatience. He turned away from the coroner, muttered, "Disgusting bird."

"Mr. Phelps," Coroner Webb said, "your opinions are of no consequence here. And if you're referring to me as a Beak—"

"No sir," Mr. Phelps said, taken aback. A look of fear pinched his face. "I call the woman a bird."

"You, sir, are the one lacking respect," the coroner said.

The foreman stood up straight, composed his features. "Yes, sir," he said, looking Mr. Webb in the eye. "My apologies, sir."

"If you please, Mrs. Wigden…" the coroner droned.

"Spend my days taking care of my children, don't I?" Mrs. Wigden said, nodding her head, "washing, cleaning, feeding…. No time for anything more."

She looked around the court, perhaps seeking sympathy. The faces of those assembled betrayed nothing.

"Though I thought we had enough kids," she said, "Gordon would come home from his labors and want to, well, you know…. Didn't matter he were filthy from his excavating jobs—he works for the Great Western Railway. He wouldn't take no for an answer."

Some of the jury chuckled. Their mirth wilted as Coroner Webb turned his stern, blue-eyed gaze on them.

One of the Juryman asked, "Could you have had less children? Could you stop now?"

Mrs. Wigden seemed to think about that for a moment, then said, "Gordon says to me, 'I work hard and have but one pleasure with you, and I mean to have it.' Yes, a good wife and mother, I am."

Coroner Webb addressed the jury. "Please allow her to finish her tale before asking more questions." He gestured toward the witness. "Please continue, Mrs. Wigden."

"I cannot look for a position for all the work I have taking care of my children. Our single room cannot hold all of us at meal times. The older children eat in the small, paved yard behind the lodging house, when weather is good. Most of us sleep in the same bed, a puzzle of heads, trunks, and limbs we have to work out each night. Some of the older children sleep on the floor under the bed.

"My cousin, Adel, and her husband, Roderick, both work at night. They rent our bed for daytime use, so I have to be quiet and keep quiet the children too young to have anywhere else to go. Sundays Adel and Roderick don't work, and should they drink, they end up in the bed with us at night. To make room, more of the children have to sleep on the floor. Often the worse for drink, Adel and Roderick are not the most careful. Half-asleep, we all shift to make room. We didn't know she suffered. My sweet bairn, Sarah, had no room to breathe. Nor did she have the breath to complain."

Mary Ann Wigden fell to weeping.

A Juryman whispered to the foreman.

"Ask her," Mr. Phelps told the man.

"Could you have slept with the infant in a chair?" the juryman asked.

Mrs. Wigden mopped away her tears with a threadbare handkerchief taken from her sleeve. "Should I fall asleep in a chair, I fall out of it, not least because I'm knapped again. Doing so while holding the bairn, I might have harmed her and the unborn."

Mr. Phelps, his features strained, had a look suggesting he suffered physical discomfort of some sort.

"Have you thought to have your husband wear a sheath?" the same juryman asked.

"We are not here to make sales for the chemist," the coroner said.

"Could you not find a bigger bed or add one?" another juryman asked.

"We cannot afford the nethers on a larger room," she said, "and without that, we cannot add another kife or fit a bigger one."

"This shifting, then, is the culprit," the foreman said all in a rush. Now, he moved about as though he had an upset bowel. "And since most, if not all, were involved unknowingly, not one person is at fault."

"Your opinion, again, Mr. Phelps?" Coroner Webb asked.

The foreman nodded and, looking sheepish, stepped back. He leaned against the dark wood paneling of the wall like he wanted to disappear into it.

A great flatulent odor rose up. A few members of the jury coughed. Others took on a sour look.

Coroner Webb shook his head, determined to ignore the gaseous interruption. "You have my sympathy, Mrs. Wigden." he said. "As a caution, I'll say that in future, you should not allow drunkards to share your bed. Should I see you again under similar circumstances, I will consider bringing the full weight of the law to bear."

He turned to the jury. "I offer my conclusions." Coroner Webb held out a single folded leaf of paper.

The foreman, head bowed, came forward to accept it.

Fifteen minutes later, the jury returned a verdict of Accidental Death.

The coroner concluded the proceedings at the Coroner's Court.

10-Samuel and the Stranger
1905

My foot in agony, I rose out of sleep and tried to dismiss the odd dream.

I felt a powerful hunger, as though more time had passed than one night. I called out to Mum, and she didn't answer. Possibly she had gone out. Daylight leaked into the room around the edges of the curtained window. Was daylight when I arrived, too.

I wanted out. With the door to my room locked and bars on the window, I felt hopelessly trapped. The window sash painted shut, I'd have to free it before I could start on removing the bars, and I had no tools. The small plot of land the house stood upon sloped down on the side that held my bedroom, which placed the window at least fifteen feet above the stairs leading down to the area. So even if I got the bars off, I'd likely hurt myself further trying to make that drop.

No, I would not get out without help. To escape the hunger and pain, I decided I had to find sleep again.

And now, I feel my right leg adrift in chill water. I cannot tell if it is a different dream. Though bound in cloth, the foot and toes feel pebbles, the slime growing in the water, and then a firm gravel slope what stops my leg from drifting. I feel the slimed roughness as my knee rubs up and down against the small rocks, rising and falling with the water.

I hear children again. They play and laugh. I feel a sharp stinging, as of small stones striking my flesh.

A man's voice, "You boys, stop that."

The pelting ceases. The giggling voices retreat into the distance. A rustling and splashing. That leg too is lifted from the water, and I feel the warming sun.

Again, I rose from troubled sleep. My hunger had grown much

more powerful. And again, I had to wonder how much time had passed, how long I'd been asleep. No light from the window.

Did Mum intend to starve me?

I called out for her over and over, got no answer.

The pain in my foot remained, yet had lessened somewhat, perhaps only because I ached so with hunger.

My thoughts still stood with one foot in slumber. I wondered about the dream woman as if she were a living person. Where had she grown up? Did she have family? How did she end up in the river? Although what happened to her could only be a dream, I could not shake the impression that I had known her thoughts and feelings, as though, while sleeping, I had become her.

Foolishness!

The pain in my foot grew large again. I squirmed in my cot, unable to find any comfort. In those endless moments, I imagined the pain to be so powerful that others nearby might feel it too. *One of them might take pity*, I told myself, *and bring me something to ease the pain*. Rubbing the gray splinter Margaret had pulled from my ankle, I wore a deep groove in the nail of my right thumb.

Again, with time, I slept.

11-The Burial Man
Holborn, London
1869

SUICIDE NOTE PRESENTED AS EVIDENCE AT THE INQUEST INTO THE DEATH OF MR. MATTHEW WHITE, CORONER P. BARNES PRESIDING

I offer apologies to family and friends for this violent act I have carried out against my own person. I cannot live with what I've done, though it started innocently enough.

My good Lord, infant life insurance was just another program sent down from the board of the company to boost our flagging sales. I had no notion what would come of it.

Earning by commission and wanting to advance, I eagerly sold the new policies. One penny per week with a minimum of thirteen weeks. Who could say no to that? Although the payouts upon death were small, nothing is too small for the desperate poor. Indeed, the product became very popular, as I'd been told it would be.

The very day the Credential Insurance Company asked to celebrate me as top salesman of the program, a friend of mine in the actuary department alerted me to a troubling increase in the infant mortality rate in London. He told me that the increase began with the advent of infant life insurance. The promised payout, it seems, has occasioned the murders of countless infants.

The majority of cases the police bring against the suspected murderers are not proved. Killers get away with the crime because most are pathetic women that juries have difficulty convicting. Once the murderers are freed, the insurance company rewards them with the payout. It is all beyond reason! The company might as well celebrate me as their top baby killer.

Now that I know the consequences of selling these policies and want to do something to stop it, I'm not allowed to see the chairman of the company. Those in management accused me of looking for trouble and have warned that if I persist, I'll be sacked.

Priscilla, when I told you about it, your outrage crushed me. I cannot stop thinking about the look of hurt and fear in your eyes as you took up our infant and fled. How I've tried to explain since, but you won't hear me. Though we've had our marital difficulties, surely you don't believe I am a danger to our sweet Pru.

The only way to be heard, it seems, is to put it in writing, and so I have. Still and all, I cannot endure the shame.

Please forgive me, Priscilla. When you remember me to our daughter, give her my love.

—Matthew White

Mrs. Ezrie Pia gave testimony that she had found the note on the street in Holborn, not far from the deceased's home. Coroner Barnes pointed out to the jury that the note bore pin holes that corresponded to holes in the breast of the deceased's blouse, and the fact that most every window of the deceased's home had been opened, allowing wind to pass through it. Matthew White's widow, Mrs. Pricilla Dovecote White, identified the handwriting in the note as belonging to her husband.

The jury returned a verdict of Death by Suicide.

12-The Stranger and Samuel
Wapping, London
1905

The cruel dream I cannot escape has me spread over several bends of the River Thames, parts of me lifted by the tide and placed on solid ground. A dog has dragged some portion of my trunk into the shrubberies of Battersea Park. Once the parts are out of the water I begin to lose the sense of them.

And I know with a certainty that I do not dream. No escape is possible because I endure somehow, somewheres between life and death.

The threat that poses brings with it a great formless fear—fear that I am formless, that I have no worth, that I have no more part to play within all of Creation. Am I no longer welcome among the living and the dead? What a terrible notion....

I must not lose my head!

That would be funny, if not for the sense that my head is all what's left of me.

For days, I am caught up in a tangle of rubbish held against a row of rotting wooden dolphins. Since there is no traffic here, the boats and ships on the Thames must no longer use these piles.

The water in my ears keeps me from hearing the city above. I do not breathe, swallow, or blink. My jaw does not move. I taste the water—not a good thing.

Small life plucks at my skin, my ears, lips, nose, and even my eyes. I cannot complain, though I want to with all my heart. My sight suffers until I can see but an occasional glow of light, as the sun and moon come and go.

I am made small. Almost gone, yet not quite.

Having slept fitfully for several days, pieces of the dream coming to me every time I found slumber, I'd long since begun to suspect they were more than mere fancy.

At least the dreams of sharp teeth had not returned.

I awoke one night, restless within damp bedding. A fever. I'd grown hot and slick with sweat and now I shivered in the chill room.

Again the hunger pangs and the ache in my foot.

Mum had left a plate on the bedstead that held a meat pie and some dried fruit—no doubt from street vendors. I stuffed all of it into my saucebox.

Still no answer after calling out for Mum several times. I thought I heard a startled female voice somewhere in the house, but it wasn't Mum.

Again, I considered working on freeing the window sash, what tool I might find or make to help me get through the bars, and the drop from the window to the ground. And, again, I dismissed the idea as foolhardy.

Rubbing the gray splinter with the nail of my left thumb, my thoughts returned to the woman I'd been getting to know in sleep.

She'd protested that she could not escape a cruel dream.

In slumber, I could not escape *her.* Awake or asleep, I'd found my-self trapped with women I wanted to get away from.

Worst of all, a terrible dread crawled beneath the strange woman's thoughts. Though I did not understand the source of that fear, I knew I'd have to face it too, should I keep finding her, should I keep *being* her.

Still, to escape the agony in my foot, I had no choice but to try again for sleep.

13-Inquest into a Death from OverLaying, Coroner J. Webb Presiding
Wandsworth, London
1870

Coroner Webb had difficulty restraining his anger as he presided over an inquest into the over-laying death of yet another of Mary Ann Wigden's infants.

In the year since the last case involving the woman, she had grown thinner. Offering few emotional expressions, the skin of her face looked thick and hard, giving her features a cold aspect. Her appearance and manner did not encourage trust.

Coroner Webb considered that the coldness might be a consequence of suffering as easily as it could be a reflection of criminal cunning. Even so, he struggled to find charity within himself for the woman.

He felt foolish, and thought of the word, *mark*, used on the street to refer to someone gullible enough to be the victim of a cheat. Had she duped him? He realized that during the earlier overlaying case with Mrs. Wigden, he'd been unable to think of her as a swindler. How would she have gained financially from little Sarah's death, beyond saving the funds that would have been needed to raise the infant? That seemed hardly worth the risk.

Even in the midst of his self-recriminations and his suspicions about Mrs. Wigden, he reminded himself that the poor got more than their share of burdens in life. He continued to believe that the majority of over-laying deaths were not crimes, but instead a tragic consequence of the rampant poverty in the city.

Yet even if she'd been innocent in the earlier case, the experience she'd had with the inquest ruling might have given her the impression that chance favored her getting away with the latest tragedy as well. His investigation had uncovered the fact that, this time, she had an infant life insurance policy. The previous night, in a discussion with his wife, Sephie, he'd been reminded of the initial circumstances that brought Daisy into their home. Much like Miss Amelia Hewiston, the woman who had first promised to care for and then killed Alice Sutton, Mrs. Wigden stood to collect five pounds should the death of the child in question be ruled an accident.

So many infants died at the hands of their parents or other caregivers, primarily for reasons having to do with depravity or economic instability, most commonly through poisoning, drowning, or bludgeoning. Those cases were harder to face, but easier to solve. The difficult ones to unravel involved infants killed by methods meant to mimic accidents, like overlaying. Just the simple act of feeding a newborn adult food, something they cannot digest, often went unnoticed. When such a cause of death was uncovered, the person responsible might claim ignorance of the danger. Coroner Webb had heard one mother say that she'd done her best to feed her infant. "His belly's full, ain't it?"

Whatever the truth about little Sarah Stahl Wigden, he couldn't help imagining Mrs. Wigden laughing about the "Gulpy" coroner who let her go. He pictured her telling her friends and family, "And he'll let me go this time, too."

Both his trust in his own judgement and his good will toward his fellow man had been wounded.

Coroner Webb referred the new case involving Mrs. Wigden and the death of her infant, also named Sarah, to the police. He would have done the same with her husband if he had not died of a burst appendix the year before. The loss of her husband had possibly contributed to the strain that drove her to the crime.

No, such speculation is not warranted, he decided.

Even so, he couldn't help thinking that Mrs. Wigden would hang for her crime. He struggled to find that charity in his heart for her, and again had no success.

One saving grace came to mind: Since 1868, executions were no longer public events. She would at least be spared the greater humiliation.

Continuing to feel the fool, he grew angrier with every step he took toward home in Churton Street, Westminster.

14-The Stranger and Samuel
Wapping, London
1905

A storm in the night, perhaps, and I am washed out of the tangle at the dolphins. I tumble through the water, strike the riverbed and something heavy comes to rest on my chin, breaking it into two parts. My head is up-side down against the bottom. I feel stones against the back of my scalp. The hinges let go and the parts of my jaw fall away. With time—I cannot say for certain how long—gravel, sand, and mud settle around me until I'm certain that I am buried.

And I find that possibly I am not alone. Somewheres in the gravel near-by, I sense an old, angry presence. Most troubling and disheartening, we cannot speak to one another. I can but feel something of the other's thoughts, a maddening jumble of scabby notions and moth-eaten memories.

Then again, I might well be describing myself, as I am angry and my memories confuse me.

Am I alone, after all? Is the other in the gravel a phantom?

Time will tell. Though, if I am fortunate, there may not be much of that left for me. Slippery things pass into and through my skull, stealing bits of me as they go. Once I have been emptied and all what's left is bone, surely then I'll cease.

I awoke to find my left foot missing. Foolishly, I looked around the room for it, all the while becoming more upset and alarmed, knowing who took it, and the likely reason.

How could an infection have grown in me so swiftly?

Mum must have returned as I slept, dosed me with chloroform, and performed the amputation.

I could not help thinking my life was over. A young man, just six-teen years, I couldn't imagine living, as so many did, without two feet to stand on.

Trying to feel better, I thought of Bartholomew Bertelson, and his ability with a sword. He had not allowed the loss of his leg to keep him down. But then, he'd taken to begging, so, however he saw himself, employers saw less and wouldn't hire him. He had also abandoned his wife, possibly fearing he'd be a burden to her.

No, that didn't help me feel better.

Weeping, I failed to hear the key turning in the lock and the door opening.

Mum entered. "Stop your blubbering."

I could not. I wanted to kill her, to rob her of the life she'd taken from me. Then I had the strangest urge to savage her with my teeth.

Mum stood away from my cot, as if sensing my desire to bite. She poured an amber liquid from a small bottle into a spoon. "This will help ease the pain." She held the spoon out so I had to reach as far as I could to get it. My fumbling fingers took it and she let go. The spoon slipped from my grasp and fell to the floor.

"Why?" I screamed at her.

She picked up the spoon and poured out another dose of the liquid.

"You gained a fever on the third day after your injury."

I didn't believe her. "How many days have I been here?"

"A week."

I tried to remember, but my memories had become so mingled with those of the woman in my dreams, I didn't know the truth. Grudgingly, I chose to believe Mum.

"Your wound began to suppurate. By the sixth day, it smelled of French cheese. Gangrene. It had to be done."

She came close enough for me to easily reach the spoon. I swallowed the bitter medicine. She set the bottle and a pipette to dispense the medicine on the bedstead. I read "laudanum" on the label.

Mum checked the dressing on my ankle stump, then left the room, locking the door behind her.

What need did she have for that?

Heedless of what Mum would think, I wept myself to sleep like a small child.

15-Stanley
Westminster, London
1870

Father arrived home from work in one of his rare, unpleasant moods, but how could Stanley have known how violently he'd react to hearing about Daisy's real secret, or how bloody the outcome?

Following the grisly spectacle, Father ordered both children to bed without dinner. Stanley and Daisy obediently retreated to their room, washing and dressing for bed silently, the events they'd just witnessed having stricken them dumb.

Rat pups with naked pink bodies and sightless eyes squashed flat like fleshy grapes. The mother rat, her muzzle stained and littered with scraps from the pups she'd already eaten before being stomped to jelly under Father's great, black boot.

The gruesome memory temporarily silenced Stanley's grumbling stomach, and as he pulled the blankets up to his chin, he once again found himself so angry with Daisy he wished she'd never been born. Daisy had been the one keeping a rat as a pet. A *pregnant* rat! All he'd done was tell the truth. He'd merely done his duty as a good son. All he'd done—

Stanley's indignation bled away as Daisy approached. Instead of sitting on the edge of his mattress as she did almost every night, she got down on her belly and wriggled underneath the bed frame. Moments later, Stanley heard a high, wet sputtering sound issuing from the darkness beneath him.

Crying?

Daisy Sutton *crying?*

The anger curdled like bad milk in hot tea, sickening Stanley's stomach. He'd never made a girl cry before, and though he'd relished the thought of causing Daisy grief, now that he'd succeeded, Stanley just wanted it to end.

"Daisy?"

More crying.

"Daisy, are you hurt?"

Foolish question. She'd curled up under his bed crying—of course she'd been hurt. Mother had gone out, so she would hear about what happened from Father. Not wanting to risk additional punishment should Father hear, Stanley slipped out from beneath the covers and sat on the floor beside the bed to try to calm Daisy. He traced the pattern of the floor's wood grain with a finger while trying to decide what to say.

"I'm sorry," he said, finally. "I didn't mean to...I-I didn't know. I didn't know he'd do...*that*."

Stanley's apology only made things worse. Daisy's crying grew louder, her sobs like those of a baby.

He looked around the room for inspiration, desperate for something to say that might lessen her anguish. Stanley's eyes fell upon the stack of books on his desk. He thought of the girl as extraordinarily clever, and realized that his envy of her natural intellect was at least partly to blame for the situation. Perhaps he might appeal to her sense of reason.

"She deserved it," he said. "She killed her own babies. You saw. You'd meet the same fate, should you ever do what she did. Father has had women imprisoned or hanged for just such an offense."

His words seemed to do the trick. Though her sobbing softened, and Stanley no longer worried that Father might hear them, Daisy made no move to crawl out from beneath his bed. Stanley thought she might have cried herself to sleep. Yet, before he could rise and get in his bed, Daisy spoke in a voice low and measured.

"She didn't have a choice."

"What did you say?" he asked, certain he'd misunderstood.

Several minutes passed in which Stanley again began to think Daisy had fallen asleep before she replied, "She didn't want her babies. There was never enough for all of them. She did what she had to do to keep living. I tried to help, but it wasn't enough. I didn't wish hard enough."

A hand, small and pale in the moonlight, snaked from beneath the bed, surprising Stanley as it found and took his own.

"I don't want to be like her, like my mum. I want to have a choice."

16-The Stranger and Samuel
Wapping, London
1905

Days, weeks, months, years. Who can say. Aside from an occasional chill or warm spell, and the murmur of meaningless thoughts from my phantom in the river bed, there is little here in the dark to mark time passing.

Memories are still hard to find and put in the proper order, yet they remain with me and I've had some time to sort them. A few are almost too painful to recall. Those about Joseph leave me feeling foolish and fill me with shame.

He were good to me at first. Quick and clever, with a satin voice, he charmed me. Joseph promised to make my wish for a home and garden outside of London come true. "There's a place for us near my family in Devon," he'd said.

"How will we ever earn enough," I asked, "A convicted absconder, you will find little but hard labor."

"I have a gift for words," he said. "Say just the right thing and people are forgiving."

Joseph give me a brass ring, said, "Hold that as proof of my love and a promise that we will be married one day. Until then, no one need know we are not wed."

He gave his most winning smile, and I believed him.

The throbbing stump of my left ankle had poured puss while I slept. I awakened to a bad smell and a wet, slippery mess at the foot of the cot.

The gray splinter rested on the bedstead, the bottle of laudanum, half-empty, standing beside it. I had no way of knowing how often I had taken the medicine because, like the woman in my dream, I didn't have a way to gauge the passage of time.

17-Stanley
Westminster, London
1881

Stanley searched everywhere for the missing anatomy text, knowing all the while he hadn't simply misplaced the book, before finally giving up the hunt and making his way down the hall to Margaret's room. Daisy Sutton, the odd servant girl turned sibling and sometimes academic rival, had adopted her more mature-sounding given name when she'd made up her mind to follow Stanley into medical school. Truth be told, it had been Margaret's unflinching will and fierce compassion that first inspired Stanley to pursue the healing arts.

In addition to the grown-up moniker, Margaret had also adopted the habit of lifting Stanley's medical texts to familiarize herself with the material in preparation for her own studies. She often returned them with notes scribbled in the margins that Stanley found quite insightful and had, on more than one occasion, helped to clarify for him concepts that his own instructors could not. In those moments, he marveled at her brilliance. That stirred within him an appreciation of her not at all brotherly.

Still, a world of difference stood between familiarizing oneself with models and diagrams of the human body and the actual practice of medicine. Tending to the sick and infirm would never be pretty, nor did it smell particularly nice. Although she, herself, had come from squalid beginnings, Stanley didn't believe Margaret capable of flourishing within such conditions again. Nor did he wish her to. She'd already endured repeated rejection from dozens of institutions, each denying her admittance on the basis of gender alone, and the last thing Stanley wanted was for Margaret to suffer the same prejudice from the very people she intended to help.

Heart thumping in his chest, Stanley knocked briskly. For the better part of a decade, he'd thought of that door as the little Sutton girl's door, because to him, that's who she'd always been. Even after Father declared her a proper and permanent part of the family, it had never been suggested that the little Sutton girl would ever be the little Webb girl.

"Good morning, Stanley." Margaret said in a clipped voice upon opening the door. Her cheeks flushed, and eyes slick with either rage or despair—Stanley could not tell which—she thrust a trembling hand into the hallway.

Stanley took Margaret's balled up fist, holding both the hand and her gaze as he coaxed the former open. For the briefest second, Stanley fancied the crumpled white ball resting in the palm of her hand as a wadded crust of bread. He imagined they were children again and he had a chance to do things differently, to spare the little Sutton girl her experience with The Night of the Rat, as he'd come to think of it. But it wasn't a crust of bread, and they weren't children anymore. Stanley could no more save Margaret from the hurt inside that envelope than he could undo his actions on that night a decade earlier.

Stanley's heart sank. He'd seen the letter resting on the dinner table the night before, when he'd returned home late following his prosection for the incoming class's first lecture at the Westminster Hospital Medical School. He suspected immediately the small envelope contained a single sheet of paper bearing bad news—not just bad, the *worst*—and he had hoped to catch Margaret that morning before she'd learned of the latest, and final, rejection.

"That's all of them, then?" he asked, as though saying the worst out loud somehow lessened its impact.

Margaret nodded almost imperceptibly.

"If it were my decision," Stanley began.

"But it *isn't* your decision!" she cried, pulling her hand away and leaving the crumpled paper in Stanley's gentle grasp. "And I don't wish for it to be your decision! I wish for my life to be one of my own design!"

Since Mother and Father had both left the house early—Mother to attend an ailing aunt, and Father to work at the Coroner's Court—nobody in the home objected to Margaret's outburst.

Stanley had long suspected that this sort of reaction from Margaret—the smoldering anger she worked so hard to deny—was the very reason she'd failed to gain admittance to university. Many, including their parents, viewed that anger in her as part of the driving force that gave rise to Margaret's compassion and made her so intellectually formidable. Though they might not admit it, he believed his parents, as tolerant of Margaret as they'd always been, considered her outbursts as unbecoming a lady.

"You don't understand what it's like," Margaret said. "You have *choices*. You could change your mind about medicine tomorrow, and the consequences would be naught."

"I wouldn't."

"You could marry, father a dozen children, and then walk away with ne're a care for what becomes of the woman and children left behind."

"I would never—"

"But you *could!*"

"No!" Stanley said, the repudiation so firm Margaret fell into shocked silence.

In the aftermath of The Night of the Rat, Stanley had lent himself to Margaret's rage, encouraging her to speak more, to share with him her true thoughts and feelings, as she had done that night. She'd been slow to open up, yet the more she talked, the more Stanley had understood the little Sutton girl and her motivations. He'd studied Margaret over the years, just as he'd studied history, science, and maths. He'd studied her for so long, Stanley secretly believed he knew Margaret better than she knew herself. This would not be the last time he'd have to endure the brunt of Margaret's misplaced anger.

She had taken a step back, as if unsure she wanted to hear what he might say next.

"No," he repeated. Softer this time. "I couldn't." He mirrored her steps to maintain the distance between them.

As ever, Margaret never dropped her gaze.

"I could never walk away from you," Stanley said.

She took another backward step, the wariness and anger in her eyes giving way to what might have been bewildered comprehension. Then she straightened and, acting as though she'd just opened the door and the previous exchange had never happened, Margaret asked Stanley, "Was there something you needed?"

He'd come for the anatomy text and the single sheet of paper tucked inside, but Stanley discovered he no longer needed any notes. He already knew what he wanted to say.

"You think I've got choices?" Stanley said. "I've got no choice, not when it comes to you."

"What are you trying to say?"

"I love you, Margaret. I love you, and I want to marry you."

Silence.

"If the decision belonged to me—" Stanley began.

"But it isn't your decision," Margaret said, her voice soft and contemplative.

"No, it isn't my decision. It's yours. And I want you to know that no matter what you decide, I'll support it. I won't stop loving you, and I won't pursue you further, either."

For the second time and for a brief moment, Stanley fancied they were children again. Margaret stared, eyes probing and wary, as though she knew something he didn't know. As if she evaluated him, comparing him to...what? She seemed to stare for a long, long time. At last, she said, "Three conditions."

"Three?"

"Yes, I'll marry you, Stanley Webb, on three conditions."

He nodded, having decided he'd agree to any terms she might set.

"I've grown accustomed to having my own chamber. Should we be wed, I wish to keep a room of my own."

"Of course."

"Having children must be at my own convenience," she said, finally taking a step forward and closing the remaining distance between them.

"And the third?"

"I wish to continue my studies. If you wish to marry me, you must promise to share everything with me, and teach me what other men will not."

∝

18-Wedding Reception
Westminster, London
1882

"If you'd asked me ten years ago, I should have said that Daisy would bring the Webbs nothing but grief," Abigail Renton told her mother.

Persephone Webb—who close family called Seph or Sephie—couldn't remember the mother's name. She had overheard because Abigail, trying to make certain her nearly deaf mother understood, had chosen to speak louder during a brief lull in the conversations surrounding her. Perhaps sensing that the mother of the bride had also heard, Abigail glanced across the dining room to give Sephie an apologetic, sheepish look.

Persephone Webb gave her a warm smile in return. She'd heard it all before and always found herself sympathetic to the point of view.

Earlier, she'd overheard her young nephew, Master Charles Webb, talking to his sister, Caroline. "...when ten years old, Daisy called down a rain of twigs from a clear sky on a paved lane with no trees."

Sephie had missed what led up to the statement. Even so, she knew the story of how the neighboring children rumored Daisy a witch, a hurtful time for the girl, odd as she may have been.

Standing near enough to the boy to hear, his grandmother, John's Aunt Ester, had taken the pipe out of her mouth and said, "Twigs might be blown anywhere." A rumbling cough followed her deep, sandy smoker's voice.

"Might be..." Master Charles said, adding sand to his voice to mock her.

Aunt Ester slapped him on the back of the head hard enough that the boy stumbled forward and dropped his plate of cake on the dining room rug.

Molly, the housemaid, hurried to clean it up.

"That's what you get for spreading lies about someone," Aunt Ester said.

Looking chastened and embarrassed, the boy had left the room, his sister following.

Sephie, herself, had held reservations about Daisy, but out of respect for her husband, John, she had done her best to set aside her misgivings—so many of them—as they occurred.

I need to stop using the nickname and think of Daisy as Margaret, as she has requested.

As a child, Margaret had been odd, especially in her early childhood: secretive, reticent, often expressionless for days on end. She did not play, even when around other children. Margaret had never come to her stepmother for comfort. Thinking about the girl through the years, remembering so many painfully sober moments with her, Sephie could not remember ever having seen her adopted daughter cry.

And she'd had plenty to cry about—at first a stranger in a strange house, then the loss of her mother, and, long before he took a romantic interest in Margaret, she'd had to contend with a brooding, conniving older stepbrother who looked for ways of scuttling her relationship with his parents.

And the predilections of the girl, herself! Sephie remembered Margaret's interest in the hunting techniques of spiders and the way she talked about them. "They bind up their prey in the finest silk and leave them trapped, yet alive, in their webs." Along with her words, she offered a mischievous smile. "Should the spider grow hungry, it bites into the head of its trapped prey and sucks out the juice." She'd giggled, and Sephie let out her own giggle, forced as it may have been.

The girl had been trying to shock her foster mother. She did not know that Sephie had once worked in the morgue where she'd met John Webb. Not much of life and death truly shocked her.

Although little Margaret shied away from others, and seemed to reserve her caring for the smallest and most helpless of creatures, the girl's tender feelings for that life, odd as it might have been, had sustained Sephie's need to care for her and to consider her family.

With that in mind, on the day she discovered that Margaret had taken several felt hats out of storage to raise "moth babies," Sephie had calmly explained that she would prefer not to have moths about the house because they ate holes in wool clothing. The girl seemed to accept that and stopped her breeding program. The hats, the worse for wear, went back into storage.

John had once frightened Margaret as she'd witnessed him killing a litter of rats and their mother. She would have been about nine years old. Sephie didn't understand all of the circumstances because she'd been out at the time. John, it seems, had found out from Stanley that Margaret had taken an interest in the rodents in the cellar. Stanley had told Sephie that his father had been in quite an upset state as he returned home that evening. She knew to leave him alone when he became that angry. She had never dreamed that his anger might get the better of him around the children.

The next evening, during dinner, John had spoken to Margaret. "I'm sorry for what I did to your rat mum and her babies. Because they are unwanted guests in our home, I did not understand how much you cared for them. Can you forgive me?"

Margaret nodded, while her eyes remained wary and full of unease. Even Stanley seemed ill at ease.

"Sometimes adults do things they regret," John said, "and the only way to help make it better is to apologize. Also, I have an idea I think you will like."

Margaret didn't ask what he meant, merely sat passively at the table, picking at her food and eating little. Though bedtime hadn't arrived, when dismissed from the dining table, she ran to the room she shared with Stanley. Sephie would find her asleep in her bed later, the children's entomology book she'd been reading still held in one hand.

"What's your idea?" Stanley had asked his father.

"That's a surprise," John said.

Sephie expected a jealous response from the boy. Instead, his face brightened and he smiled.

Over the next few nights, in the workshop of the area, John built a trap to capture a rat alive for Margaret to keep as a pet.

A week later, he surprised her with the rodent.

"I shall call him Percy," she said and smiled, an unusual thing for her. She reached a finger to touch the rat through the wire bars of its cell.

"Stop, dear," Sephie said, "You must agree to never get close enough to him that he could bite you. We don't know what diseases he might carry."

Margaret pulled her finger back and nodded.

"You will keep him in your *new* bedroom," John said.

The girl's eyes opened wide and her smile grew larger.

"We've cleaned out the guest room for you," Sephie told her.

Again, she expected Stanley to react with envy, yet he did not. *Extraordinary!*

She looked to her husband, said, "That has the added benefit of saving us from having to allow an overnight guest."

John's cousin, Harry, a drunkard, showed up on their doorstep unannounced, looking for a place to stay, whenever he came to London.

"Keep Percy in the trap for now," John said. "while I build his palace."

She picked up the trap and hurried toward the stairs to go to her room.

"Don't run," Sephie said. "You might drop it and hurt Percy."

Margaret slowed, glanced back with a grin, and mounted the stairs, fairly tiptoeing in an exaggerated show of care.

Using wood and strong wire, John built a two-room cage with a doorway between that could be shut. Margaret employed a little cheese to lure the rat from one room to the other once a week so she might clean his living quarters. After the creature had gone through the door, she would shut it. Percy went back and forth, from room to room, for the rest of his life, which was not long because Margaret overfed the poor creature.

One day, Sephie saw a deep cut on the girl's right index finger. Margaret admitted that the rat had bitten her, and that it happened as she'd tried to pet the animal.

Stanley, always interested in medicine because of his father's work, had cleaned and bandaged Margaret's finger. He monitored its progress until she had healed.

Realizing she had no way of knowing where the rat had been and what diseases, if any, it carried, Sephie had waited on tenterhooks for the finger to become infected. Luckily, Margaret healed up well and quickly.

Those events had been the beginning of a change in her, and, oddly, a change to a more caring Stanley as well.

Sephie's good friend, Simpka Weis, approached and took her hand. "A good thing you two gave Margaret her own bedroom," she said. "Who could have known they would grow up to fall in love and be wed?"

Sephie put a hand to her mouth, pretending the idea had scandalized her, then gave a broad grin. "Yes, we did so just in time, it seems."

"How is Stanley getting along with his position at the Westminster Hospital's medical school?"

"His future looks bright. He's been there almost a year, and he likes the work." Sephie lowered her voice and gestured for Simpka to lean in. "You know that Margaret was not accepted to any of the medical schools, so Stanley has taught her on the side ever since he started his own medical training. He believes he can get a medical degree for her from Scotland. Margaret has professed a desire to help women through charitable endeavors. The newly-weds will return to sharing the room they'd had as children until Stanley can earn what they'll need to set up their own household."

"Well done, Seph," Simpka said.

"I have done little. They are both headstrong and have done well for themselves."

"You raised them."

"I suppose I did."

Sephie watched Margaret from across the dining room. Standing with Stanley and smiling, she appeared to be happy. The wedding ceremony and reception in the Webb home, which included close to forty guests, was going well—not too crowded as John had worried.

Stanley's loving, contented gaze followed Margaret's every move, even as he spoke with the guests, laughed at his friends' jokes, and partook of the delights Agnes, the cook, had prepared as reception fare. Sephie chuckled to see Stanley pluck a candied cherry from the slice of cake he held on a dish and almost drop it before offering it to his bride's smiling mouth. Margaret accepted the fruit delicately, then kissed Stanley.

The woman in the beautiful wedding dress—modeled loosely on Queen Victoria's wedding gown, but with less crinoline and more bustle and decorated with Irish lace—bore little resemblance to the sad girl, Daisy, who had come to live with the Webbs at age seven.

19-The Stranger and Samuel
Wapping, London
1905

Foolish, I were, to pretend to be Joseph's wife. And worse, to stay with him after he began treating me rough. The day he learned I'd become knapped, he left me to attend business in Devon and didn't return. I couldn't pay the nethers and lost our lodgings.

Were in the streets of Lambeth, Battersea, and Wandsworth for many days, a month or more, a miserable, hungry time. I took what small work I found, mostly small factory labor. Got nothing regular worth the doing for the pay.

On off hours, I begged.

Whilst some beggars saw me as a threat, most of them treated me with care. Several of them defended me when one tried to scare me away. I have few complaints about the poor.

Those who could afford to give me a little something often treated me unkind, a few unabashedly so. "Undeserving," some said of me. One woman kept her companion from giving me a single farthing, saying, "She looks like one of the undeserving poor." I'd heard that sort of thing said before I became a beggar, and had never truly thought about it. The people who say such a thing must believe there are those who don't need to beg, and do so anyway to gain extra funds. But who are they, these swindlers with so much time on their hands, and how can one tell, since those who do sorely have need also employ dodges to encourage pity? With positions of employment hard to come by, is it any wonder there are so many needy people? I'd say that those speaking of the undeserving poor must themselves be undeserving.

Though I wore the brass ring Joseph give me, those who guessed rightly that I were an unwed mother, scorned me. Most often, if given anything, it'd be advice that I should seek relief at the workhouse. Yet I knew better than to enter those dark, Satanic mills.

"You're bleeding, love," a beggar named Poppy told me.

A warm day of rain, I hadn't noticed the wetness in my skirts. We stood near the Sheep Pond at the eastern edge of Battersea Park. I backed up against a tree behind me. Poppy followed with a caring look and offered me a rag.

"I am six months gone," I said, as if that explained the problem.

"And that's not a good sign," she said.

I took the rag and wet it in the pond, then went to the public urinal in Queen's Road to clean up before returning to Poppy.

A worn-down woman in her middle years and thin as a rail, Poppy wore clothing in such disrepair she struggled at times to keep them on. "Think of it as a costume," she'd said of her clothing. "I work the shallow. That's a type of beggar what gains sympathy looking so poor she cannot even clothe herself." She'd taken me under her wing to teach me how to beg. She told me about all the other types of beggars and their fakements. I trusted her.

"A female surgeon named Peg takes what she calls 'constitutionals' in the early afternoon here in the park. She'll know what's best for you. If I see her, I'll point her out to you."

"I'd be better off should the infant die."

"Will likely die whatever you do. But you don't want to be carrying a dead child, and it's too late for a simple abortion. You are young and have your whole life ahead of you."

"I am twenty-one years old."

"Yes, very young. Find Peg and ask for help. She's no lady and not a nice woman, yet she has medical training and knows how to help women in trouble."

"I cannot pay her for the service."

"Promise her anything, then abscond. Plenty of places she'd never find you. She can't take it to the police."

Thereafter, I spent my days wandering the paths of Battersea Park begging, approaching women walking alone, and asking for Peg. I got the oddest urge to sink my teeth into some of the men and women who scorned me.

In the evening, just before the gates were shut for the night, I'd hide. Sleeping rough among the shrubberies in the park should have been worse, but for the warm nights. To avoid fights, I had to be careful not to take up in a spot already claimed by another person sleeping rough. In nightmares during that time, I chased after John, trying to bite him. Toward the end of that string of dreams, I threw him to the ground and bit open his neck, killing him. That both thrilled and alarmed me.

When finally I met Peg, she did not look the part. I shied away.

"I assure you, I can help," she said, taking my hands. Whilst to see her face did not comfort, the warmth of her hands did. I wanted to trust those hands to unburden me. "Are you married, have a common law arrangement, or are otherwise involved with a man?"

"No. I am alone and have been sleeping rough here in the park."

"Two nights from this one," she said, "Monday, come to my home, a house, number 19 in Globe Street, Wapping. Arrive before nine of the clock and take the stairs to the right of the house down to the area."

"I've nothing to offer in return."

"You will work for me for a year to pay the debt. I will provide bed and board."

A position in a household? *I thought.* No, more of an indenture. *No matter—I had nothing else. "Yes, I can do that."*

"Good," Peg said. "Just lost my last slavey and need a new one."

"Lost her?"

"No, not like that. Her contract had run its term and she left to be wed."

Felt a bit better to hear that.

"You're not to tell anyone anything about me or what we're doing. Do you understand?"

"Yes."

"And I mean nobody." *She gave me a stern look.*

I nodded.

"What is your name? Just your given name."

"Elizabeth."

Had Mum known Elizabeth? No. More foolishness. Knowing Mum's trade and finding myself trapped in her house under her care, I'd merely dreamed the two women together.

With Elizabeth's desire to bite, I feared my dreams of snapping teeth had returned.

I'd got too pissed on laudanum to make sense of any of it. Instead of using the pipette to take drops of the medicine, I'd taken to sipping from the bottle.

Like the dream, Mum had come and gone while I slept. The mess at the foot of the cot was gone. The bed clothes had been changed. A new dressing had been applied to my ankle stump. The jerry had been emptied and cleaned, as had the basin. The ewer held fresh water. The gray splinter still rested in its spot on the bedstead.

20-Snatched

Stepney and Wapping, London
1883

Darkness once induced a state of suffocating fear, one never entirely conquered in life, but in death, the swaddling gloom is like unto a mother drawing a newborn to her soft breast—a profound stillness in which you had finally found peace.

With time, that peace is disturbed. Beyond the dark, a voice grows steadily louder, the muffled sounds sifting through the overlying earth to collect in your dead ears and become words.

"…are the twins who pegged out on the same day. Me and Devlin are thinking we'll get them both with half the toil since they're buried together in a large coffin in Kensal Green Cemetery. We get there only to find a mortsafe stands in our way. Devlin goes off his head, banging with a pickaxe on the iron bars. I'm not having any of it and leave. Later, I learn Devlin were arrested and sits in gaol. Some time after that, he got four months hard labor for his trouble. Never saw him again."

The speaker, an unsophisticated man of the street, drunkenly and bitterly laments several other new burial fashions intended to thwart bodysnatchers.

"Allow me to dig for a while, " comes a young lady's voice.

"Your husband has hired us to do the work," responds a third. "He wouldn't want to see your fine clothes dirtied." He is another man of the street, his rough, gravelly voice much closer as he digs in the pit just above your head and shoulders.

"'Twas my husband said I had to get my hands dirty."

"They're dirty enough, Margaret," comes a younger, more gentlemanly voice.

"What's more," says the close, gravelly voice, "we're deep enough, almost there."

A sharp sound, as of something hard striking the lid of your coffin.

"There, you see. Rusty guts, grab the brace and bit and get in the pit."

Heavy feet strike the coffin lid, followed by the sound of an auger being set, and the grind of it penetrating soft pine.

The sweet smell of pine pitch touches your withered nose, and chips of wood fall onto your lifeless neck and chest.

Scant light filters in as the man above moves about. Finally, he crawls out of the pit and you count a line of ten holes. Something metal bangs against the head of the coffin.

"Hand me the rope," says Gravelly Voice.

A grunting from above, and then a sharp cry.

"Do you need help," the woman asks.

"No, ma'am," says Rusty Guts. "Had my appendix out and it's still sore."

The grunting resumes with the sound of the coffin lid popping and creaking. Creaking becomes cracking, and the wood breaks away jaggedly along the line of holes.

One of the men leans over to look into the coffin, turning a bullseye lamp on your face, brutally banishing the darkness and stealing away what remained of the peace it bestowed.

"I thought you said we were going after a haybag. This one here, he's a cove."

"'Tis a woman's name on the marker, ain't it?"

Yes, the wooden cross not only marks Elles's grave, but the epitaph gouged into its surface stands as your final effort at poetry.

"You know I can't read."

The other two men and the woman appear on either side of the man with the lamp.

"Stanley," the woman said to the younger man, "you, too, said she'd be a woman."

"That matters little for our purposes," the young man says. Despite his words, he looks dismayed. "Let's get him to the house in Globe Street."

Gravelly Voice lifts you enough for Rusty Guts to slip a rope under your head and chest and up through your arm pits. They climb out of the pit and each grab an end of the rope. Hauling away on it, they lift your body, head and shoulders first, from the coffin. Once you are free, they lift your body into the trap, while Stanley holds the horse's bridle to keep the vehicle steady. Gravelly Voice sits in the driver's seat, Rusty Guts beside him, and drives the trap out of the cemetery, Stanley and Margaret, following on foot. Rusty Guts turns and throws a blanket over you.

$$\Rightarrow \text{※} \Leftarrow$$

Death had its beauty, and never more so than when it came for Elles.

Suffering consumption, the young Belgian woman appeared as thin and pale as a girl half her age. Flushed with fever, her lips were as rose petals, her cheeks like cherry blossoms. And, oh, how exquisite your unexpected love for her. Unlike several women you'd known before Elles, her affection did not seem dependent on the allure of your inheritance.

"My future is today, for I have few tomorrows," she'd said as you lay together in bed in the flat in London you used when slumming. Both muse and mirror, she had the ability to reflect the devotion she inspired, but perhaps no more than that.

She introduced you to the deathless words of Keats and Shelly, awakening within you a desire to compose poetry—a desire eclipsed only by your adoration of her. Indeed, what little success you enjoyed in publishing you owed to that yearning laid at the foot of her throne.

Her favorite line from Keats, *Darkling I listen; and, for many a time, I have been half in love with easeful death*, exquisitely expressed your feelings for her.

Then, as if your entire courtship had been nothing more than the brief and blinding moment Elles first appeared in your life, she was gone. In grief, you drank away the vestiges of your inheritance while returning nightly to the cold earth beside her grave, desperately inviting Death's cold kiss.

Yet when that kiss came at the end of a grave robber's spade, you were surprised.

You had come to the graveyard as you had for many nights. This time you found a lone bodysnatcher violating your beloved's grave, a slovenly fellow who reeked of cooked cabbage and sour whiskey. He did not look formidable, and you challenged his claim. He didn't even look up before turning and swinging his dirt-crusted blade.

The woman named Margaret stands over you as Stanley converses with the other men in the next room.

"Did you know Elles de Bray?" she asks you.

Hearing her name again is nearly enough to reignite your cold, dead heart, though not for the reason you expect. If you could but speak, what curses you would heap upon your beloved's memory. You tried to follow her, and for what? Your shared love of death did not survive the grave, and your efforts to rescue Elles from the desecrations of medical men doomed you to share her fate.

Every day begins the same: Margaret and Stanley arrive, he offers her instruction for an hour, then leaves her with specific tasks and goals. Today she removes your heart. Traitorous organ that it is, you are relieved to be rid of it.

She turns to look you in the face. "I know this isn't what you thought life after death would be, and I'm sorry."

She thinks you can hear her.

No, she thinks you can't hear her, the bitch.

She holds your heart in her hands, enumerating as though for your benefit its various parts and their functions.

"Blood enters the heart through the vena cava, passes through the right atrium into the ventricle through the tricuspid valve, then passes through the pulmonary valve into the pulmonary arteries, through the lungs, and reenters the heart via the pulmonary veins. From there, it passes from the left atrium, through the mitral valve into the left ventricle, and leaves through the aortic valve."

Smartly, she says nothing of love.

"Ellis is beginning to reek beyond my ability to cope with it," Margaret told Stanley one morning as they entered the surgery.

"Who's Ellis?" he asked innocently.

"That's what I named our house guest. You know, from the name on the marker."

She mocks you.

"I named mine Perceval, Arthur, Frederick, Charles, and Edward after past prime ministers. They were kept chilled when I wasn't working on them, so I didn't suffer as much as you are."

"On the day you proposed hiring the resurrectionists," Margaret says, "you said we couldn't get a cadaver from the hospital because the Home Secretary guarded them jealously. I didn't question that, yet it seems odd."

"The Home Secretary has an Inspector of Anatomy who knows the whereabouts of all available cadavers in London and who are the teachers and students working with them. We simply can't work within that apparatus, since you do not have a license to practice anatomy."

"I thought, since you are a prosector at the hospital, you might just slip one in your pocket before coming home one day. Aren't I the foolish one?"

"Well, yes, you are." Stanley laughs and Margaret giggles.

To beat back the odor of your decomposing flesh, Margaret has today brought a sachet that depends awkwardly beneath her nose from a string looped around her ears.

"You'll have to learn to live with it a bit longer." Stanley says. "The smell will only get worse. Today you're going to extract his lower alimentary tract."

"Ah, shit," she says with a grin.

"Exactly."

Surely you feel more discomfort from witnessing this glimmer of their love than Margaret suffers from inhaling your stench. You can but silently suffer her trespasses.

Leaning over your hollowed out chest, her sachet falls free and tumbles into the coagulating ooze that has gathered in the sanctuary where your heart once preached the virtues of love.

"I told you that wouldn't work," Stanley said, snatching the sachet and tossing it to the floor.

"Should we have gone somewhere other than a pauper's cemetery, he might not smell so bad. He stank fresh from the grave."

Little does she know from what pedigree you spring.

"Just like we're all pink on the inside," Stanley says, "we all rot the same, rich or poor. What we present on the outside is what matters in life."

Later, following Stanley's departure, Margaret seems lost in thought while grappling with lengths of your distended bowel. "What do you think, Ellis?" she asks. "If we're all the same in death, does it matter how we present ourselves in life? Does that presentation survive when the rest is nothing but corrupted sinew and bone?

"We pulled you from a paupers grave," she says, "smelling like the wretched beggars on the street. If a man's soul were a lump of viscera, would yours look much the same as Stanley's?"

➣ ❀ ➢

A month later, she isn't as curious. She is thoroughly disgusted with you.

"Ellis, I do this to learn what I must in order to help women. If not for the rigors of motherhood and the controlling nature of their men, some might use their energies and intellects to better themselves. Why are you making it so hard on me?"

As though you have any choice in the matter. Certainly no more choice than do most women when it comes to pregnancy. Does she think this is easy for you, watching yourself being taken apart?

A knock on the door interrupts your useless invention of insults that will never be delivered.

Reginald Black, you may recall as Gravelly Voice, one of the two men Margaret and Stanley employed to fetch you from the grave, stands in the doorway. "When you're done with him, Ma'am, me and Paul McAlhaney are ready to help further."

McAlhaney must be Rusty Guts.

Mr. Black smells nearly as bad as you do. Margret takes a step back.

"And why would I need your assistance?"

"Well, the body will need to be in pieces, wrapped in cloth, and tied with string before we dump them in the Thames."

"Why are they wrapped?"

"Should they be seen floating downstream bundled in cloth, they will not raise an alarm without being captured and opened. There's so much rubbish in ol' Father Thames, most don't pay heed to something like that."

"I see. Rest assured, my husband will contact you should we require your services."

After Mr. Black has gone, Margaret returns to the surgery. "Did you hear, Ellis? Those men want to chop you into pieces and throw you in the river."

For a brief moment you think it's possible that she's not the witch she seems to be.

"And deny me the pleasure of doing it myself? No, I'm owed that."

Yes, she is that witch.

You hate her.

꧁

21-Elizabeth
The Thames foreshore, Wapping, London

Peg's house in Globe Street, much like her face, did not encourage. I stopped to get a better look, still not quite certain I should go through with what I'd planned. The abode had not aged well, the stained weatherboards in front warped, several eve brackets and part of a window frame missing. A stiff wind rattled the window panes as I approached. Close up, I saw that most of the paint had peeled up, making a texture something like scales, the wood beneath silvered and cracked. That house hadn't seen servants in many years. Even so, I found the area entrance, and knocked.

I did not wait long before Peg answered. "Come in quickly," she said. As I dithered, she said, "Quick. Hurry up." She grabbed the collar of my coat and yanked me inside, slamming the door behind me.

Seeing that I didn't take that well, she said, "I apologize for treating you that way. I have nosey neighbors."

I stood huddled into myself, looking around. The floors and walls had not been cleaned for some time, and a pong of rot came from somewheres within. Trying to be hopeful, I forced myself to step away from the door and into the room.

I thought again of the warmth of Peg's hands, and followed her. We passed through a kitchen in disuse to a scullery with a long table, no doubt once used for food preparations and cleaning. The table had numerous three-foot rolls of fabric, like bolts of cloth, set together in rows forming a bed of sorts. The windows, set high in the wall at the far end of the room, had been covered. Peg had placed several lamps and two mirrors at one end of the table. A long counter to one side held sets of tools I didn't recognize and two basins, one full of steaming water. Some of the tools had a look what frightened me, but I chose to believe she would use them to help me. Though a stove in one corner had given the room a welcomed warmth, I shivered and quaked as I pushed down on my fears.

"Take your clothes off and lie on the table," she said.

The rolls of cloth were more comfortable than I'd feared.

She gazed down on me with a frightful look, and my fears got the better of me. When she turned away to fetch something, I sat upright, having decided I would not go through with the abortion.

She turned back with a piece of cloth in her hand what had a pleasant, sweet smell. "No one will find you here," she said.

The words did not put me at ease. I swung a leg off the table edge to reach the floor.

She lifted the leg and pressed me back gently with a hand to my right shoulder.

I tried to quiet my trembling.

"No need to worry any longer," she said, and held forth the cloth to my face. "Smell this. It will help you relax."

22-Margaret
Wapping, London
October, 1884

Walking to her Globe Street surgery, Margaret encountered a familiar face.

"Miss Peg, a moment please. 'Tis Siobhan."

Margaret stopped and turned. She had performed an abortion for the Irish woman a week earlier.

"Do you have a little something for me?" Siobhan asked. "I ain't had nothing to eat for a day and more."

Margaret took a step back. The other woman smelled like death, like Ellis.

Long after Margaret and Stanley had dumped the pieces of Ellis in the river, the cloying pong of his rotting flesh remained. She smelled it while in crowds on the street and in the cramped spaces at market, where she was forced to mingle in close quarters with the poor. The odor wafted from their clothes and mouths as though their very souls had rotted. She tried to remember if she and her mother had ever smelled that way.

Recently, she'd had to keep reminding herself to be sympathetic toward the women she treated, knowing that their circumstances were often beyond their control.

If not for the Webb family, I would have been just as wretched.

No, Mum and I never smelled like that—not like Ellis.

Stanley had said, "We're all pink on the inside, and we all rot the same, rich or poor."

Perhaps he merely meant that we are all equal in death.

Still, every time she got a nose full of death, like she did from Siobhan, her compassion wavered and her distain for the poor grew. Hadn't Stanley also said that how we present ourselves is what matters?

Surely the poor wretches could do better, but they don't try. They remain obstinate; content to beg, always taking and never contributing.

"I'm sorry, Siobhan," Margaret said. "I've got no coin to spare."

"No chink? You're a *liar*. I ain't blind. I see your clothes. Nobody works for free what ain't already rich."

Margaret stepped past the woman to continue toward the house in Globe street.

"How dare you turn your back on me!" Siobhan shrieked. "You made out what you was different. You only pretend to care. You're no better than the ponces and Peelers!"

At that moment, possibly drawn by the commotion, a constable turned into the street along the footway. He approached Margaret and asked politely, "Excuse me ma'am, is this woman giving you trouble?"

"Yes!" Siobhan offered, "I loaned her a florin yesterday, and she promised repayment today."

The constable pointedly looked Siobhan up and down and then Margaret.

The Irish woman wore her skirts hemmed up high to show her ankles, and her blouse loose enough that the smooth valley between her breasts might be seen. Locks of her hair hung from her coiffure and dangled provocatively from beneath her bonnet. Her profession could not be more obvious.

In contrast, when the constable looked at Margaret, she knew that he saw a proper woman, all buttoned up, nothing out of place.

The policeman asked her, "Is that true?"

Margaret looked back at the wretched woman, and felt a pang of pity. "Yes, sir." she said.

Clearly pleased with herself, Siobhan held out her hand to receive the coin.

Seeing the smug look on the woman's face, Margaret's sympathy evaporated. She produced two shillings from her pocket and tossed them into the street atop a fresh pile of horse manure.

"Don't mistake this for truckling," Siobhan said, stepping off the kerb and reaching delicately to pluck the coins from where they had landed. "Though I kneel to pick them up, I bow and scrape for no one."

Margaret shook her head. *What a mouth she is.*

"Has that settled the matter," the constable asked.

"I'm satisfied," Siobhan said.

"Then be on your way."

"Thank you, sir," Margaret said.

She brooded all the way to the surgery. Although she wanted to remain compassionate toward Siobhan, the woman had made that impossible. Margaret had helped her end a pregnancy that would have brought the woman much hardship, and yet she wanted more. Margaret's desire to help those less fortunate had been seriously tested.

April, 1885

About to turn the key in the lock on the area door to close the Globe Street house for the night, Margaret heard an unfamiliar male voice. A policeman? She turned slowly, trying to keep her composure.

The owner of the voice stood nearly as tall as Stanley's six foot frame, but the comparison ended there. While Stanley's clothes always fit well, this fellow bulged out of his, the cloth puckered up around the few buttons remaining on his jacket, his patched trousers, with a split seam, seeming to hang from only one hip. Gnats buzzed around his head of untamed black hair. His jowls sagged from his jaw like those of a hound dog and waggled as he spoke. "Are you the one they call Peg?"

"Are you the new rag and bone man?"

"I'll take that as a 'yes.'" He reached past her, turned the doorknob and forced her backward into the house.

Margaret retreated into the old kitchen to put distance between them, and turned her fiercest gaze on him. "If you're here for money, I don't have any."

"Well, that's too bad because you owe me."

"We've never met. You must be mistaken."

"You harmed one of my girls. She's been laid up for a month since you made her unpregnant."

Nearly a month earlier, a young woman named Agatha had returned shortly after the procedure that ended her quickening. She complained of abdominal pain and heavy bleeding. Margaret had examined her. She wasn't bleeding at the time, so Margaret had given her a placebo with instructions, and sent her on her way.

During her studies with Stanley, Margaret's work with the male cadaver had taught her almost nothing about the anatomy specific to females. Instead, she'd turned to medical texts to learn more on the subject. She believed abortion should be legal and that it should be performed with strict standards to make it safe. Stanley remained on the fence about abortion, though she'd worked hard in their discussions for several years to win him over to her way of thinking.

Impatient to begin offering abortion services before she'd practiced on a female corpse, Margaret leaned on her ability to learn quickly, taking the chance that, when problems arose in the procedures, she would recognize them and find solutions. Yet now a problem she did not foresee had caught up with her before experience could complete her education.

Hubris, she told herself, *and now I'll suffer for it. Who is she to this man?*

"Is Agatha your daughter?"

"Would that she were," he said, chuckling. "Nothing that pretty would come from me."

What then, a wife?

No, he's letting me know he's Agatha's ponce.

He closed the door behind him.

Margaret took the chance to retreat into the surgery where she picked up a Liston knife from off the table. He entered, saw the knife in her hand. In the midst of a great belly laugh, he pulled his own blade, one eight inches long and much broader than hers. Margaret's heart sank.

Struggling to hold herself steady, she set the Liston knife back on the table and asked. "What do I owe you?" She realized she'd grown much more angry than afraid.

"Half quid."

"Tomorrow," she said, trying to match his manner of speaking.

"Not tomorrow. Now. Tomorrow you could be gone."

"There's no money here. If you've asked Agatha, you'll know I don't charge women for my services. My work here is charitable."

"That's all well and good, but mine is not. If you don't have the chink, I'll take from you the way I do my girls: a pound of flesh."

Margaret heard the area door open and she cried out, "Help me, please!"

In response she heard fast-approaching footsteps. Agatha appeared behind the man, craning her neck to see around him and grinning.

"Can I watch, Dog Face?"

"Yes," he said, and the beating began.

Agatha laughed throughout the ordeal.

When Dog Face Dowd and Agatha had gone, Margaret heaved her aching frame from the floor and let out the wail she'd held back while being beaten. She stumbled to the basin, removed the towel draped over it, and splashed water on her face. Reaching for a standing mirror with her right arm, a deep, sharp pain told her the limb had been broken. A bulge along the curve of her ulna suggested the break was singular and complete. Nothing could be done for it at present. She'd have to see a bonesetter.

With her good arm, she positioned the mirror so she could see her face. No damage there. No doubt the man called Dog Face excelled at causing his girls pain without damaging their most alluring feature. Good. That would make it easier to lie about the circumstances of her injuries. Perhaps he'd become as skilled at his trade as Margaret had at hers. That gave her an idea.

Margaret moved to the cabinet in the corner of the surgery, took a bottle of laudanum and a pipette from its second shelf. She measured out five drops of the tincture and swallowed them. Gathering her blue and green woolen shawl from where she'd dropped it in the kitchen during her retreat, she fashioned a sling and carefully slid her aching forearm into it.

Winchester

At the front door of her home in Warwick Street, Margaret reached for the keys in her top skirt pocket and realized she'd left them in the surgery and had fled without locking up. Hopefully no one would try the door before she could get back there.

When Stanley answered her knock, she donned the role of victim and sunk to her knees.

"Oh, Stanley," she said, "he took everything."

Stanley's eyes grew wide and he crouched to help her stand.

"Mind my injured arm," she said, twisting out of the grip he took on her right shoulder.

"What happened?"

"A terrible man beat and robbed me. Send Hildegard for the bone-setter."

Stanley guided her to her room and helped her onto the bed, then left to speak with the housemaid.

Margaret released her arm from the makeshift sling. Squirming to find a comfortable position, she tried to picture her assailant, or at least the one she'd tell her husband about.

"Do you know who he is?" Stanley ask as he reentered her room.

"No, I've never seen him before."

"What did he steal?

He never comes to the house in Globe Street anymore. He'll never know the truth.

"All of it," she said. "Since I had no money for him, he took my instruments. I'm so sorry I couldn't stop him."

"You *tried* to stop him?"

"Yes, that's how I got harmed."

"You should know better," Stanley said, slowly shaking his head. "You've never known when to back down."

His concern is turning to anger. Good.

"I can replace your instruments," he said. "I can't replace you. Perhaps it's time to start charging for your services. You wouldn't have to charge much to weed out the undeserving. If you'd had funds, you could've given that, kept your instruments, and avoided injury."

She gave him a doe-eyed look, accentuated by her slight laudanum intoxication. "You may be right, Stanley, but what would have stopped him from taking both the funds and my instruments?"

He seemed to have no answer for that. His anger dissipated. Stanley pulled a chair from the corner of the room and sat in it beside her bed, holding her good hand, head bowed in silence, seeming defeated.

"He was a big Scottish fellow," Margaret said, "with ginger hair and beard, dressed in a brown and black checked suit. His clothes being fresh and new, I thought odd for a criminal. He hit me with a neddy."

"A what?"

"A weighted stick."

Stanley looked up with a grimace.

Once she'd finished her story, he gave her hand an affectionate squeeze. "Should we inform the police?" Something about the way he asked the question, she got the impression he knew she didn't want the police in her business.

"No, I don't want them any where near the surgery."

"I'll give you funds to replace your instruments. Start charging and I'll find a gater for the house."

Margaret feigned delight and said. "I know just the right person. He's rough, but so much the better, and the women, rough as most of them are, won't care."

Stanley stared at her for a long moment. As a worrisome look took hold of his features, Margaret got the sinking feeling that she'd revealed too much of herself. Quickly, she took on a bright smile, said, "I won't apologize for being ambitious," then she laughed like a little girl.

Stanley responded with the adoring gaze he'd been giving her ever since she'd won his heart. He smiled and they laughed together. Yet, as he left the room, she saw his face reflected in the mirror—that worrisome look had returned.

~ ~ ~

Shadwell
May, 1885

"It's nothing personal," Dog Face said, rolling up his sleeves. "It's just business, like when we did her." He gestured toward Margaret, who stood on the third-floor landing, just outside the door to Agatha's single room. The prostitute couldn't escape.

Even so, she made as if to dash past Dog Face. He grabbed her by the hair and brought his fist to meet her face. Her mouth went sideways as it sprayed red onto the upholstered chair to her right.

"You said you'd never hit me in the face," Agatha sputtered, spitting blood.

"That's when you were in my employ. I don't need you bunters anymore. I just accepted a respectable position."

Other women perhaps hearing the violence—more prostitutes by the looks of them—emerged from their rooms onto the landing.

Margaret gestured toward them, said to Dog Face, "They're watching."

"Don't worry," he said. "I'm invisible."

Does he really believe that? How could that be true?

The other women huddled together behind Margaret, trying to

look over her shoulder to watch Dog Face go to work on Agatha.

Margaret had thought she'd enjoy seeing the woman beaten. Instead, she winced at the wet crunch of Agatha's nose splitting and breaking upon her former ponce's fist. The sound reminded her too much of the sound of rat pups popping beneath a large black boot. Still, once the pounding ended, and Agatha lay bleeding on the floor, Margaret felt herself smile and couldn't help thinking, *She deserved it.*

The River Thames
March, 1888

Dowd is smart to remain silent, Margaret thought. *I don't need another man to manage my affairs.*

The death of her client, Francesca, had aroused anger deep within her, and the feeling wouldn't go away. The woman was the first of Margaret's clients to die from her procedure. Under normal circumstances, she might confess her feelings to Stanley, but given the fact that she'd killed a woman, if accidentally, that wasn't an option. Margaret didn't quite know what to do; many years had passed since she'd felt so alone.

She faced Dowd as he sat aft in the dinghy, rowing slowly to make little sound, his gaze moving to take in everything around them. In the foggy gloom, his silhouette looked like that of great beast, its breath puffing out white plumes in the chill air.

He is a very quiet, calm bear. My bear. Should we be discovered, he'll do whatever he must to protect me—in truth, to protect his income.

Three of the clock in the morning, she'd met him below the Wapping Old Stairs. He'd been right: With the tide coming in at the time, few visited that stretch of foreshore.

"Hurry," he'd said as soon as he and the boat came into view through the fog.

The boat hesitated and ground to a halt in the gravel and mud. She waded out into six inches of water and climbed the two-stair jetty to stand slightly above the dinghy's gunwales. Dowd extended a hand, and she stepped into the vessel, careful not to walk on Francesca, who lay in cloth bound pieces against the hull in the bottom of the boat. Margaret could make out a couple of slim fingers poking out of the cloth wrapping of one of the parcels.

When she'd dumped Ellis in the river, she'd had Stanley's help.

Without Dowd's help, she would have had great difficulty getting this far with Francesca, and though Margaret wanted to show him gratitude, she couldn't quite bring herself to do so.

She looked back with shame and a sense of helplessness on her night struggling to save Francesca's life. The woman had begun to bleed during the abortion procedure. Margaret had failed to locate the site of the bleed and stop it. Once the hemorrhage had killed Francesca, Margaret had felt absolutely worthless. Then came the anger that wouldn't let up. None of that sentiment truly involved Francesca, who she did not know in any significant way. Margaret might have responded the same way to loosing one of her favorite dahlias in the back yard garden at home. Something about what happened seemed unfair, as though Margaret herself had somehow been cheated.

Such cold, heartless feelings!

Where is my concern for the woman?

She tried to console herself with the idea that maintaining objectivity helped keep her feelings from getting in the way of her work.

No, I just don't have anything for her.

"Leave it with me," Dowd had said as she'd brought up the disposal task and said she'd go with him.

"No, should I find difficulty in it," she'd said, "I will work harder to avoid such a terrible outcome in future."

Dowd's brow had furrowed and his eyes had squinted up hard as he stared at her. He clearly had difficulty understanding what she meant. Yet he didn't question her.

Having him in her employ, she'd learned that he was good at recognizing when she'd made a decision and didn't want to consider the matter further. He also kept his opinions to himself. Dowd never once raised doubt about her being the boss. She liked that about him.

Once seated on the forward thwart, Margaret's concern about being seen increased. Dowd used an oar to push the boat off the gravel as he got them moving downstream. What illumination reached them had been filtered through the fog. Much of that light seemed to float by just above the surface of the water in the distance. She could just make out the silhouettes of other vessels, some large, some small, just beneath the floating lights. She heard voices here and there, coming out of the fog as if from nowhere, sometimes startlingly close, or so it seemed. Turning to find the owner of a voice, she might see nothing but fog. Other times, she'd see someone piloting a small boat tens of yards away. She came to understand that the fog carried sounds unevenly, some boosted, others muffled. Margaret snuggled into her shawl to push back the chill trying to spirit her warmth away. She hated the fog and the smell of the river water.

Even though the poor visibility helped protect their anonymity and purpose, she feared their endeavor might be exposed. What if the River Police stopped them and inspected the boat?

Dowd seemed to be at ease. She remembered that when she'd gone with him to punish Agatha, he had not been concerned that the other women in the building might see him beat the prostitute. "I am invisible," he'd said.

Did he truly believe that? Had he made a wish much like those Margaret made? No, more likely his reputation for brutality made people think twice about reporting his crimes?

Watching him take his time, rowing slowly, his gaze untroubled as he maintained awareness of their surrounding, she could readily believe he truly thought of himself as invisible. She wanted to share that confident outlook.

Margaret considered making her own wish for invisibility. In the past, the wish came first, then a death. *But now there has been a death, so can I pin one to that? Or am I putting the cart before the horse? What does it matter—no one will try to stop me.*

"I wish that all I do in my services to women will be invisible to the police," she whispered.

"Pardon, miss?"

"I was wondering if you put anything in the parcels to make them sink."

"No, because they don't always stay sunk. We want the current to swiftly carry them downstream. The farther the remains get from us, the harder it'll be for the blue bottles to link us to the poor woman."

Did he chuckle? Had he made a joke? Margaret tried to see his face, but shadow obscured her view.

No, you are still angry and looking for reasons to justify it.

After a time, Dowd said, "We're close to the center of the river, where the current is the strongest."

He glanced about as he reached for a parcel and slipped it over the gunwale and into the water silently.

An arm, a leg, a section of trunk? No, the one with the fingers sticking out is missing. That must have been it.

Following his lead, she lifted a parcel and quietly fed it to the river, then another, and another. They were heavier than she remembered. Within a short time, all of Francesca had gone overboard.

Even with the task done, Margaret's unease would not lift. Yes, she'd found the task difficult, yet not in the way she'd expected.

As long as I do the work, there will be the possibility that my clients will die. Knowing that, I will always carry the feeling that one day I'll be exposed. That could mean prison or hanging.

Why can't I just be sad over the tragedy of the young woman's death?

A steam-powered whistle blew some two hundred yards away. Startled, Margaret let out a short, sharp cry. She watched Dowd, expecting he might smile or even chuckle. He did not.

"Take me back as quickly as you can."

"Yes, Ma'am."

Invisible indeed!

Wake up, Margaret, you are no longer a child.

23-Elizabeth and Samuel
Wapping, London
1905

That were all until a pain in my gut awoke me suddenly and I cried out. Peg reached a bloody hand with that same cloth toward my face, and I knew I had to fight. Something or someone told me to bite her. I went for the part of her I could reach, and bit off the last joint of her left pinky. Then she were on me, pressing the bloody rag to my face, the look in her eyes pure rage.

"You ungrateful—you want to join Francesca?"

I knew no more until I found myself in pieces in the river.

I awoke to the murmur of female voices in the old servants area below my room, an echo of what I'd just endured. I recognized what I'd seen in the dream as the area where Mum plied her trade. Not mere dream, what I got from Elizabeth while I slept seemed more like true memories now.

I sat up and reached for the laudanum on the bedstead, a new, full bottle, and almost dropped it upon seeing that, not only was my foot missing, the lower leg below the knee had been taken away as well.

She's doing it again—doing it to me.

I'd got pissed on the laudanum by the time Mum returned to check on me, and I pretended to be asleep, my back to her as she approached.

Kill her.

Though it sounded in my head like the same voice I'd heard at the river when I stepped on the skull, I believed it to be my own thought.

As Mum got close enough, I twisted around and grabbed her by the neck.

Quicker than I'd have believed possible, she held a knife to my throat.

I tried to let go. My hands resisted—no, *refused*. Struggling to unbend my fingers, I released her and held my hands to my chest.

She pointed the knife in my direction. She'd been smart to bring it with her.

"The infection had spread upward," she said. "It had to be done."

I nodded so she'd know I understood. "Who's here?" I asked, but she gave no answer. I took that to mean I'd been hearing things that weren't there.

Too much of the laudanum, I decided, although I didn't think about taking less of it.

"Who is Francesca?" I asked.

Mum dropped the scissors she'd just picked up, and stared at me for the longest time. Then she picked up the scissors and started to remove the bandage from my leg.

"Who's Elizabeth?"

Mum took my stump in a powerful grip. While I screamed, she gave me the most hateful look I'd ever had from her. Finally, she let up.

I wept as she inspected my stump. When done, she dressed the wound again and left without another word.

✂ 24-Stanley
Westminster, London
June 1889

"I've named him Samuel," Margaret said.

Stanley stared at the infant in his wife's arms. She pulled away folds of the swaddling, her faded blue and green shawl, to allow him a fuller view. Barely the size of a puppy, with ruddy, wrinkled skin sprouting a fine, almost transparent hair, the child had obviously come too early.

Unsure what to say, Stanley repeated the boy's name, "Samuel," as he followed Margaret into her bedroom.

"Yes," Margaret confirmed, staring deeply, earnestly into his eyes. "His mum didn't survive the delivery, and he's so tiny, Stan. I had to bring him home."

"When did you start delivering babies?"

"I haven't. It all happened so fast. The mother came to me in labor. I had to help her."

"You should have called for a midwife."

"Why, when I have the skills?"

Stanley shook his head, yet remained silent.

Margaret left the child in her bed. She emptied one of the drawers in her clothing chest and nestled a soft blanket into it. Then she lifted Samuel and placed him in the loose folds of wool.

"I must go to the area and ask for milk," she said and left Stanley standing in her room, staring at the infant in bewilderment.

After they'd wed, Margaret had insisted that, while she did desire children, she would complete her medical tutelage before taking on the responsibility of motherhood. She insisted that Stanley wear a sheath whenever they engaged in sexual congress. Stanley obliged, albeit grudgingly at first. Much of Margaret's practice consisted of helping women avoid unwanted pregnancies and providing sheaths to her clients had always been a part of that. Stanley believed such precautions should be reserved for those who hadn't the means to care for offspring. If Margaret hadn't told him years earlier, on The Night of the Rat, that she wished to have a choice of when to become a mother, he might have grown angry with his new wife.

Two years earlier, when Margaret had decided she was finally ready to have a child, they dispensed with using the sheaths, and with time discovered their caution had been entirely unnecessary. Either Margaret, Stanley, or both had some physical problem that rendered them incapable of producing offspring.

Margaret returned with a frown and no milk. "I've sent Hildegard to fetch milk from the Johnstones."

"Have you considered this carefully?" Stanley asked, taking care to hide his exasperation.

"The thought of him ending up like baby Alice…" She held a hand to her mouth, her eyes suddenly sad.

Stanley touched Margaret's cheek as if to wipe away her tears, and felt none. He frowned, said, "He must have a family. What of the father?"

Margaret looked away. "Likely a whoremonger and the woman, his mum, a prostitute. She came to me bleeding, frightened, and alone. I didn't have time to learn her name. Not that it should matter."

Stanley's thoughts returned to The Night of the Rat. Margaret had always cared for the most wretched and undeserving creatures, so he shouldn't be surprised she'd claimed Samuel for herself. The only surprise was that, seeing as many pregnant women as she did, she hadn't worked out a way to bring home an infant before that day.

The Lord knows many a mother would gladly hand their child over to Margaret, he thought, *a learned woman with a husband and a gainful trade.*

Yet she'd waited for an opportunity to turn tragedy into triumph. After trying unsuccessfully for a baby of their own, would he begrudge his wife giving the child a better life? He would not.

Still, a sense of unease clung to Stanley like a winding sheet on the dead. Her language as she spoke about the poor had grown more callous in recent years. He remembered what she'd said on the day he offered to hire a gater: "I know just the right person. He's rough, but so much the better, and the women, rough as they are, won't care." The statement seemed a marked departure from the attitudes she'd held toward poor women in years past. He realized that, hearing it come from her on that day, he'd felt a bit ashamed of himself. *What she'd said sounded more like something I would say.*

Whilst she would never look upon the problem of the poor with the clear eyes Stanley had, he knew he'd always loved her most when she expressed her sympathy for others, even if her compassion remained misguided.

Once Margaret hired Dog Face Dowd, Stanley had vowed to stay out of her business and allow her room to develop it on her own. And he had kept that vow, although that had been difficult at times because of Dowd. He'd seen the man at a distance on the street a couple of times. On one such sighting, he'd had what looked like blood on his cuffs. In another that occurred in Battersea Park, the brute had been leaning in close to another man's face and speaking angrily, while the fellow had cowered back against a stone wall. Stanley hadn't heard anything about Dowd that didn't point to his unsavory character.

Yet, his unease was not a good enough reason to deny her wish. "Very well," he said. "We shall keep Samuel and treat him as though he were our own, same as Mother and Father kept you."

Although Margaret did not return his gaze, Stanley sensed a smile.

"Samuel," she cooed, looking down on the infant in his makeshift crib.

"A good name," he said. "God did indeed hear and answer your prayers."

Margaret shook her head and whispered, "'Twas a wish, not a prayer."

25-Elizabeth and Samuel
Wapping, London
1905

Over time, I feel the living walking above me—a few women, some men, mostly children. How I know they are there, I cannot explain, except to say I feel them thinking. The men don't hear me. The women seem to hear me and dismiss what I have to say. The children—almost all of them boys—hear me the most clearly. They seem to believe my messages are their own notions, and, on occasion, they act upon them. I've had them pick up stones above my resting place and cast them into the Thames. They removed at least some of what holds me down.

I taught three of them how to skip flat stones on the water. What fun!

When they became excited, I caught quick glimpses through their eyes: a patch of blue sky with the whitest of white, wind-tossed clouds, a ship of the line moving along the river in the sunlight, a boy wearing the green seaweed of the river like a beard and mustache.

In those moments, I tried to fix where on the river I might be. The boys lost interest in throwing stones quickly, though, and I failed each time.

Once a bright young lad come near, one with a head full of fancy and just enough room inside to allow me a peek through his eyes—one longer than I'd had with any other. Saw a house afire across the river and the smoke rising from it high into the sky. Through his ears, I heard a train whistle, the cries and songs of birds, and the lapping of the water against the foreshore. I also had a taste of his last meal, gone stale and sour on his tongue. But oh, what that did for me! Starved as I'd got for something, anything to happen, even his bitter spit were a breath of fresh air.

Then, my boy, my sweet child, he vanished.

Robbed of sobs and tears, still I wept.

The foreshore holds me down. The gravel above could be feet thick or just a few inches. I hope to be uncovered one day, though I cannot say how I would gain from that. I reside within a small bone vault what has no limbs. I cannot move. My eyes, tongue, and ears are gone.

I rose from slumber as her memory touched mine—I recalled standing on the foreshore six years earlier, at age ten, and feeling something reach inside me. With the help of my guides, Rollo, Zeb, and Gillan, I'd just gained an interest in the River Thames and the treasures it turned up. Whatever had reached into me on that day, I'd gained from it a sense of my beginnings for the first time, a wonderful, if mysterious feeling I didn't understand.

Remembering, I snuggled into the quilt, as if I might wring warmth from it, and perhaps answers as well. My bedroom held the damp chill of Father Thames, not an odd thing in that drafty old house. I'd known that particular chill most of my life.

She isn't your mother.

That thought sounded in my head almost as words. I nearly leapt from the cot.

Don't be frightened.

I'd known some on the streets who heard voices. None fared well, and I didn't want to count myself among them. I'd heard enough tales of Bedlam and the like to know I didn't want to end up with the lunatics.

You are mine.

What was happening to me?

You are my flesh and bone.

And then the thought I'd been denying: *Elizabeth is my mother.*

Gleeful, the voice inside my head said, *Yes!*

I shivered in the sweat-dampened bedding.

"Mum dismembered you and...put you in the river?"

Yes, she said, followed by such silence, I thought she'd gone.

No longer chilled, I threw off the quilt. Trying to *listen* for her, I knew her heart's desire: Elizabeth would see Mum dead. She wanted vengeance and hoped she might use me as a tool toward that end. I can't say how I knew those things except to say that it must have been much like her knowing things about me—we had somehow become one.

Whilst I heartily disliked Mum, I had no desire to see her dead. She'd changed to a cold, bitter shade of the caring woman she'd once been. Though I remained angry for what she did to my leg, I knew she'd done the right thing to save my life.

Elizabeth's memories did not show the surgery that ended her life. So many women died from that procedure, I had no way of knowing whether or not Mum had intended to harm Elizabeth. Why would she? Her job was to end a—

"You tried to have Mum kill me," I said aloud.

No answer, silence.

Did I merely talk to myself? Did I indeed belong in an asylum?

The room—again so hot.

No, I could see my breath puffing out pale vapor in the chill air.

The heat came from inside me. The fever had returned. I knew what that meant. Should the infection get to my hip, I'd be done for.

In anticipation of what was to come, I took several sips of the laudanum.

∝

26-Stanley
London, Wandsworth to Westminster
1889

"You're quite certain?" Stanley asked.

Nearly two weeks had passed since Margaret walked in through the front door to their home in Warwick Street, holding Samuel in her arms. During that time Stanley had tried to ignore the growing suspicion that his wife was withholding something. Not since The Night of the Rat had he harbored any serious misgivings about Margaret's activities, but when he'd asked about Samuel's father, she had looked away before answering. Something about that and her changing views on the poor had become linked in his mind, though he couldn't quite make sense of why that might be.

The following day she had developed a fever, and Stanley discovered an infected wound on her left hand, where the distal-most joint of her small finger had been severed. Wincing as he submerged the raw digit and nub of exposed bone into a tumbler of gin, Margaret said, "I have no memory of how I got the injury. I suppose that in my rush to deliver Samuel, my blade slipped."

The nub didn't look like it had been cut with a knife, the edges appearing ragged. Another falsehood. Why? What did Margaret hide from him?

Now, faced with facts presented at an inquest he'd been invited to attend, Stanley had grown all but certain he knew the answer. He could scarcely restrain the urge to run home to confront Margaret with his ghastly accusations, not because he wanted her to suffer, but because he needed to know the truth right away. Just the thought of that confrontation made his gut contract and eject stomach juices up into his throat. He forced the sour, biting bile and acid back down as he stood with his father's friend and colleague, Mr. Hicks, the coroner for Mid Surrey who had presided over the inquest. Dozens of other inquest attendees surged around them as they exited The Star and Garter Battersea pub.

"Quite certain, Dr. Webb. Would you care to see Dr. Bond's report?"

Mr. Hicks extended a bundle of papers, and Stanley took them. He knew he would find nothing in the pages that had not already been described in excruciating and gruesome detail during the inquest, certainly no detail to quell his burgeoning horror. Yet if he truly planned to accuse his wife of such brutality and evil, he must first read the other doctor's findings for himself. He flipped to the first page.

The victim had been recovered in pieces over a period of twelve days.

A trio of boys bathing in the Thames near Albert Bridge had discovered a left thigh, wrapped in a scrap of women's undergarment. At nearly the same time, five miles away under London Bridge, a waterside laborer spotted a parcel washed ashore that contained the lower half of a female body. The upper half, minus the head and arms, turned up two days later. One by one, pieces of the dismembered body were found washed up in Fulham, Limehouse, Vauxhall, and other locales before being delivered to Dr. Bond's examination table. Her right lower leg and foot, followed by the left. Her left arm and hand. Her right thigh. A piece of liver and several feet of intestine. Her buttocks and pelvis. In the end, only the woman's heart, lungs, and head remained unaccounted for.

Stanley didn't want to imagine what might have become of the woman's head; her death had been ugly enough without the added insult of being robbed of her identity, but as unbelievable as it may seem, worse had befallen the victim than mere dismemberment and mutilation. Stanley returned to the page detailing the most unsettling of the chief surgeon's findings:

"The uterus had been opened on the left side by a vertical cut, six inches long, through the left wall.... The cord measured 8 in. and the distal end showed a clean cut. The vessels contained fluid blood."

Whoever she was, the victim had been six to eight months pregnant at the time of her death, and the fate of the infant taken from her womb as much a mystery as the location of her head.

Stanley handed the papers back to Mr. Hicks, his hands trembling just the slightest bit.

"Awful," he said with a hand to his brow.

"Monstrous," Mr. Hicks agreed, shaking his head as he accepted the report. "And we cannot say with confidence if any of the similarly mutilated victims discovered in the last few years are related."

An odd sort of hope compelled Stanley to ask, "Might the murderer be Jack the Ripper?"

"No, the methods are too different. The Whitechapel Murderer left his victims posed and exposed for all to see. The torso murderer—as the press have dubbed the fiend—makes an effort to hide his victims."

Unfortunately, the man's quick and definitive answer put that idea to bed.

"Should you be pressed, which of them would you say are most alike?" Stanley asked, not at all certain he wanted the answer.

"The torso uncovered at Whitehall and the one from Pinchin Street. Several of those disposed of—forgive my bluntness—in parts in the river going back as far as 1873."

That year had been well before Margaret would have been capable of such monstrosity, Stanley told himself. With that, he found himself, perhaps erroneously, exonerating her from all but the most recent murder.

Then Hicks cleared his throat, and, in an obvious attempt to lighten the mood, asked, "How is Daisy? I've not spoken to her since the wedding."

"She's well. She goes by Margaret now."

"Margaret, yes, of course. I understand she has a small practice of her own?"

"She does. She distributes prophylactic sheaths and pamphlets concerning methods to avoid pregnancy, and provides light surgical services to women in Wapping." Stanley struggled to keep his tone steady and conversational.

"Ah, skilled with a knife, is she?"

"Skilled enough for the women of Wapping," Stanley said, and again, he felt ashamed of his callousness. In any case, the statement held a half truth. If not for her sex, Margaret might have become the Metropolitan police's chief surgeon instead of the esteemed Dr. Bond.

"The White Chapel butcher last fall was terrible enough, and now this." Mr. Hicks gestured with the report clutched in his left fist. "Handy with a blade or not, I should not want my missus on the streets. Margaret would do well to stay closer to home until the police catch the fiend."

In truth, Margaret hadn't returned to the decrepit building where she practiced her trade since the night she'd come home with Samuel. Her arm on the mend, fighting the infection in her finger, and caring for a premature infant had left her with neither the time nor the energy to care for anyone else.

Stanley counted backward to that night, noting the date, June 3. One night before the first of the unknown woman's remains were discovered.

Straining to do so, Stanley gave the coroner his most grateful smile. "Thank you, Mr. Hicks. 'Tis sound advice."

"Speaking of the missus, I'm expected. Good to see you, Stanley."

The two men parted company. Mr. Hicks disappeared into the groups of people still crowding the footway.

Stanley waved to the driver of an idle hansom. When it pulled up next to him, he quickly stepped up into it. As he rode across the Thames on the Chelsea Suspension Bridge, then east along Grosvenor Road, his need to confront his wife congealed into a rancid clot of disbelief and trepidation in his gut. Deciding he needed time to think, he asked the driver to pull to the kerb. Stanley got out of the Hansom in Claverton Street, paid the driver, and moved north, walking slowly and taking frequent detours.

He remembered trying to damage Daisy's standing within their childhood home, calling out, "Father, come and see the crime I've uncovered."

An inquest, a dead infant, and his need to meddle in Margaret's affairs had set the stage for blood and violence on The Night of the Rat. The sense that events were repeating themselves dizzied Stanley and he doubled over at the kerb in Charlwood Street. Unable to suppress the bile and revulsion any longer, he vomited into the gutter. Those walking along the footway gave him a wide berth.

⚹

27-Press Fragments Continued
1873-1888

Mystery in Battersea
The Thames Police gathered several portions of a young woman's body from the river near Battersea. The remains had not been divided crudely, but carefully disarticulated...
—the evening edition of *The Illuminating Star*,
September 5, 1873

Another Torso in the River
The Thames Police found the dismembered body of a young woman in the river at Putney. Because the head and several limbs are missing, it is unlikely that the corpse can be identified...
—*The Signal*, June 15, 1874

Killed by His Own Victim?
The bodies of a man and woman were discovered this morning on the Thames Embankment. Each had effected the death of the other with a knife. They lay as they must have fallen, clutching each other in the struggle that ended both of their lives. Apparently, the man had bitten the woman, a known prostitute, on the cheek. That has led to speculation that he might be The Shadwell Shark...
—The All-Seeing Orb, January 7, 1875

Mystery in Tottenham Court Road and Bedford Square
Several wrapped pieces of a woman's body were

uncovered at various locations in Marylebone, among them, an arm bearing a tattoo, which has led to speculation that the victim is a prostitute...
—The Quotidian Advertiser, October 25, 1884

Stabbed 39 Times

In the early morning hours of August 7, a man named Reeves happened upon the body of Martha Tabram, stabbed 39 times and left dead on the first floor landing of the George Yard Buildings in Spitalfields...
—The Quotidian Advertiser, August 7, 1888

✂

28-Samuel
Wapping, London
1905

Mum, looking haggard as though she had not been sleeping, was with me when I awoke. She offered me Laudanum from a spoon held in her left hand. I noticed again what I'd known all my life—the joint missing from the end of the pinky on that hand. Feeling unsteady, I held the hand as I drew the liquid off the spoon into my mouth. She moved to inspect and adjust the bandage on my stump.

Elizabeth's voice in my head said, *Kill her.*

"I don't want to," I said.

Pausing to look at me, Mum asked, "Don't want what?"

The amputation had been done above the knee this time. I shook my head, suddenly speechless.

I'll help you, Elizabeth said.

"What is your—?"

I shouldn't have said that aloud. Mum gave me a queer look, like she might have known I'd become heedful of something unseen.

What is your meaning, I thought.

Using my left arm, Elizabeth reached for the cup of water on the bedstead, lifted it, and brought it to my lips.

I struggled unsuccessfully to prevent her control, my arm shaking and spilling some of the water. Finally, with my right hand, I took the cup and set it back where it belonged. Now I knew why my hands had not wanted to let go of Mum's throat. I hid my fear and frustration.

Mum watched my uneven movements with a look of concern. "Have you had that palsy before?" she asked.

"No," I said.

Since I bit you, Elizabeth said, *I've been able to bide inside you.*

I'd had sympathy for Elizabeth. That ceased with her threat to control me. Odd that I'd been picked on for being the son of a witch, only to find Margaret is not my mother but that my true mother is indeed something witchy. Whatever I got inside me off her teeth—her thoughts, her spirit—had moved faster than the infection in my tissues. I didn't know if I could get her out. I certainly could not think of a way to go about it.

Mum had brought me another meat pie, a barmy muffin, and an apple. I couldn't remember the last time I'd eaten. I fell upon the food like an animal.

"You've been here for more than two months," Mum said. "As hard as it may be, you must find a way to get along on your own. You chose the street years ago and that has left you a cripple."

"No, *you* did that!"

"Not with your mouth full," she said in the hurried, flat way I remembered from childhood.

I spat the food at her. "*You* took my leg!"

"To save your life." With a maddening calm, she brushed the food from her clothing, face, and hair. "Shouting for me, you have frightened away clients. I can't keep women overnight with you here."

"Doesn't the padding dampen the sound?"

"You make more noise in your sleep now than you did before you left home. I have my work, and I need this room and the cot."

I swallowed what remained in my mouth. "Mum, you can't turn me out like that. Please."

"I can't put you back together either, and I cannot continue to take care of you. Another week. Should you grow worse, I'll have to take you to the infirmary at Mile End."

"The workhouse?"

"Yes."

I stared at her dumbfounded.

A few years earlier, when unwell, Mum had confided in me that, as a child, she'd feared the workhouse more than death. She'd held that fear before John Webb took her and her mum in. He'd given Mum's mother a position within his household and found light domestic duty for little Margaret as well. After her mother's death, the Webb family chose not to send little Margaret to an orphanage. No, they continued to provide her with a home. Knowing all that, seeing how her heart had turned so cold, I couldn't help hating her.

"I'll return tonight to change your dressing," she said, then paused, looking at me critically. "Your friend, Bart, he didn't seek relief at the workhouse. But like him, to stay out, you'll have to come up with a way to earn."

She would see me become a beggar. I couldn't help thinking she encouraged me to hate her.

ॐ

29-Stanley
Westminster, London
1889

Upon arriving home, Stanley proceeded directly to the basin in his bedroom, where he took a few minutes to splash water on his face and gather his thoughts. He looked into the mirror above the washstand, and wondered briefly if the one staring back at him would be up to the task at hand.

During the walk, he'd considered a dozen approaches, ranging from dropping hints to prompt a confession to simply sending for the police and allowing them to handle it. Then he imagined Margaret swinging from the gallows and nearly vomited again. No, he'd do as originally planned and ask her outright if she killed the woman, and when she denied it, Stanley would reveal what he'd learned at the inquest.

Margaret lay drowsing in bed in her room, with Samuel asleep in a new crib at the bedside. She'd removed the bandage from her damaged finger. Bloodied yet dry, it lay like a wounded white animal atop her spare pillow. Stanley sat on the edge of the bed and took his wife's damaged hand. The wound was healing nicely. Before she could greet him or ask how his day had gone, Stanley asked, "What happened to Samuel's mother?"

Margaret's eyebrows knitted together with a suspicion that infuriated Stanley. Still, he waited for her answer.

"I told you. She died."

"Yes, but I want to know how, Margaret. Just how did she die?"

Margaret sat up and withdrew her hand.

"Why do you ask?"

Stanley, unwilling to draw out the discussion, looked his wife dead in the eyes and asked, "Did you kill her?"

Margaret's face took on a grimace, as she stared at him.

She feigns speechlessness or she's looking for a plausible lie.

Finally, "How dare you—" she began.

For the first time since they were children, Stanley interrupted her, shouting, "How dare I? How dare you! How dare you use the knowledge I shared with you to take a life!"

"Like an animal, the wretched woman bit me!" Margaret shouted back, holding out the hand with the damaged pinky. "I tried to help her, and the ungrateful, miserable creature bit me!"

Despite his earlier conviction that he knew what had happened, Margaret's admission shocked Stanley to silence. He knew her lack of denial meant she admitted to the truth. But knowledge and belief being two separate things, the part of him that loved Margaret, the part of him that would have died to protect her, had steadfastly refused to believe her capable of such evil until that moment. Stanley backed away from the bed until he reached the wall. He slid to the floor, cradled his head in his hands, and wept.

He heard the bed frame creaking as Margaret rose, felt her rest a hand on the back of his neck, the skin cool and dry against his. When she'd volunteered at the hospital, he'd watched her treat countless patients in that manner, imparting comfort and calm by mere touch. He wondered if she'd touched Samuel's mother that way.

"It's not what you're thinking." If he could taste it, her voice might have had the flavor of honeyed mead. "Disoriented, she'd gone mad and must have believed herself in danger, because she became violent and bit me. I subdued her with chloroform and delivered the child. Once finished, I tended my own wound while I waited for her to awaken. When she didn't wake up, I knew I'd used too much chloroform, and…" Margaret's voice trailed off as if there were nothing more to the story.

"You stole him, then," Stanley said. "Samuel."

"His mother was *already* dead," Margaret countered.

"They discovered pieces of her mutilated corpse spread from Battersea to Limehouse, Margaret."

"I didn't mean for it to happen. I don't know what his reasons were, but Dowd secured a boat upstream, well past Battersea, and took her out—"

"No, don't tell me…!" He clutched at his head as if he suffered a terrible ache. "They found her womb empty except for the placenta. It had been cut open to extract the infant."

His wife's face became the hard, impassive visage of a little girl who'd just witnessed the demise of a beloved pet. Stanley had expected her to break down and cry, to offer some explanation that made sense and beg for the forgiveness he would gladly give her.

Instead Margaret said, "They're like rats, Stan, breeding constantly. And no matter how hard I work, no matter what I do, they keep coming back. Most women only need my help once or twice. This one came back five times! I couldn't bear it any longer!

She's lying about the woman coming for so many abortions. Stanley could not have explained how he knew that, yet he did.

"She wanted another baby gone, so I took him, and so what if I left her to bleed."

Stanley's mouth strained to speak around his outrage. "Are you saying it wasn't the chloroform that killed her?"

"Perhaps if I'd not given her so much she might have alerted me to the bleeding, but by the time I'd finished with the baby, there was so much blood and it was too late. That's not the same as killing. So, from among the countless poor, another is gone—no great loss. After all this time, I finally realized you and Father were right. I dare say she deserved it."

Her explanation consisted of a mixture of truth and lies, Stanley knew, but the last three words—recitation of his justification for the murder of her rat—could not have cut him deeper had they been made of perfectly honed surgeon's steel.

Even following Margaret's defense of the rat, Stanley's opinions of the less fortunate, and the opinions of his friends, had remained much less charitable than his wife's. On more than one occasion, she'd demanded that Stanley intervene when one or more of his colleagues or their wives, mistaking her for just another one of the girls, spoke too flippantly of Margaret's clientele. Those occasions grew increasingly less frequent through the years, and now he understood why. She hadn't merely grown tolerant of the bigoted vitriol, as he'd once thought. No, she'd grown to accept it as she, herself, had grown callous toward the poor. He'd witnessed the same change of heart within his own father.

Shame wider and colder than the Thames turned the air in Stanley's lungs to lead and the blood in his veins to steaming pitch. If she were guilty of murder, then he had been an unwitting accomplice.

"No," he said, swallowing the shame. "I suppose letting someone die isn't the same as killing."

As she smiled, he knew he couldn't stomach more.

"But you are a killer, aren't you, Margaret. Your pamphlets, the prophylactics, and small surgical remedies would never be enough. You help women end pregnancies. How long have you been at it?"

Her smile vanished. If Stanley were to taste it now, his wife's voice would have the tang of gin and bitters.

"At least five years. My work is to give women a choice. After so many clients, I've lost only two. How does that compare to the others offering the service? The first one I lost, Francesca, bled to death, though I struggled to save her."

If she'd been performing abortions for five years, there would have been more losses. Suddenly the reason she had spent the night so many times at the Globe Street house seemed to come clear: She'd stayed there on nights when she'd had a client with complications resulting from a procedure. Margaret would not have been willing to send a suffering client to hospital for fear of exposing her role in that suffering.

"Why didn't you tell me about that?" he asked.

She seemed to have no answer for him.

Since he believed she'd lied about the number of women who had died under her care, she was unlikely to countenance any questions involving more than two. He already knew about the latest. "What became of the first one?" He regretted asking that even as the words left his mouth.

"Dowd and I—"

"No, I don't want to know."

"Don't pretend you didn't know I provide abortion services."

He wouldn't. He had known about the abortions, even if they'd never spoken of it. He'd told himself he'd done that to protect Margaret, but part of him begrudgingly acknowledged the good her services did. Although Margaret had undoubtedly helped the women of Wapping, some of those women had died, and instead of behaving like a surgeon, Margaret had chosen to act like a butcher.

And while he would not turn her in to the police for the death of Samuel's mother, Stanley would not spend the rest of his days raising a reminder of his failure.

"Get out."

"Pardon me?" For the first time since he'd known her, Margaret looked genuinely surprised.

"Get out," Stanley repeated. "Take Samuel. Go to the Globe Street house. I don't ever want to see you again."

Margaret gathered her belongings, bundled up the child, and left without another word.

That night, and every night for the rest of the month, Stanley prayed for the dead woman to find peace. On the eleventh night, in a conversation with Coroner Hicks, he finally learned her name: Elizabeth Jackson.

30-Samuel and Elizabeth
Wapping, London
1905

"I want you out," I told Elizabeth, my fear of her coming out as anger.

I can't go anywhere what's not you.

"What does that mean? Why not?"

I don't know where I'd go or how I'd get there.

"Because Zeb took your skull to the Police?"

Don't know. I don't understand. Wouldn't go back should I have the chance.

"You bit Mum, uh…Margaret Sutton—you call her Peg."

Yes… You call her Mum?

"She raised me." I didn't offer more. What did it matter? Though my vexation had got the better of me, discovering that she didn't understand what was happening any better than I did told me I had to be careful not to get too huffy with her. "Margaret Sutton—*Peg*—is the one who harmed you, not me. Can you get into her and let me go?"

When you touched her hand, the one I bit, I felt a small, open passage. She will not want me any more than you do.

Feeling a darker warning beneath her words, I dismissed it as mere notion.

"That's what she deserves," I said. "I don't know if Mum killed you on purpose, but, after you died, she cut you up and tossed you in the river like you weren't human anymore. You're not the only one." Looking down at my stump, I thought, *I may be joining you soon. Parts of me might have already.*

I thought about Zeb and Gillan and how they feared Mum because she might be a witch. I wondered if they'd believe me when I told them the truth about her.

Elizabeth remained quiet for some time. I didn't know how well she knew and understood what I thought and felt.

She would send you to the workhouse...?

"Yes. I've never been anything to her but a bother, and now she's no longer pretending to care."

When she comes in to change your dressing, find a way to bite her. That might get me in. I cannot say for certain.

I looked to the bedstead, thinking about having more laudanum. My gaze settled upon the gray splinter. Mum had let it be, cleaning up around it.

No laudanum, I told myself. *I must stay awake and sharp.*

"What will you do once you're with her?"

That's not for you to know.

✥
31-Rollo
Various Boroughs of London
1905

When Sam had not returned from his Mum's house after more than a month, I worried. Because things between Margaret Sutton and me had gone sour, I sent Zeb to knock on her door.

Later, he found me at the river, trying to pull a large iron bolt from the gravel. "That'd be worth something at the marine store," he said.

"Would I be working so hard at it otherwise?"

He gave me that blabber's look of his.

"Did you speak to Sam?" I asked.

"No. His mum said I couldn't come in because he has a bad infection and needs his rest."

I cut my eyes mean at him. "Did she say *when* we could see him?"

"I *did* ask that. She said, 'too early to tell.'"

He helped me with the bolt. The thing were over a foot long and had a square nut on one end. The other end passed through a hole in a rotten ten-inch thick wooden beam of no value, buried in the foreshore.

As we worked at getting the bolt loose from the beam, Zeb asked, "Do you remember that I dug a skull out of the foreshore where Sam got hurt?"

"Yes, you said you saw Sam's blood on its teeth. You also said the skull might have belonged to a pirate hanged at the Execution Dock."

"That's right. Well, later, Gillan told me they carted away most of the dead pirates to give to the medical men."

"To be anatomized?"

"Yes. 'Most, yet not all,' Gillan tells me. 'One what I know they didn't take to the medical men was William K. Bytre. That would have been in the year 1736. Until he turned pirate, he'd been a privateer, taking prizes from the Spanish and Portuguese for King Charles. Bytre went by the ekename, Billy the Biter, because he liked to bite parts off his opponents during fights, mostly noses and ears, but some fingers too.'

"'Imagine you're a merchant aboard a ship about to be boarded,' Gillan says. 'This pirate captain and his men climb over the rails onto the deck of your ship. He smiles and you see that his teeth are sharpened to points. Around his neck is a cord strung with ears and noses he's taken in other fights. Do you want to go up against him? I wouldn't. Most wouldn't have the stomach for it.'

"Gillan said Bytre had done much worse than bite. He had a habit of cutting up captured enemies while they were still alive so they could watch him throw their arms and legs in the sea. He also gutted and carved up the faces of prostitutes what disappointed him.

"He tells me that, awaiting execution, Billy suffered a pain in the right side of his gut and they carted him from the hulk, where they held him, to a barber surgeon in Wapping. The Admiralty didn't want to give him a chance to die of appendicitis. No, they wanted to be the ones to kill him."

Zeb seemed to ponder something, then his face brightened. "'Hey, you think Bytre might have been hauled to Margaret Sutton's house? Being in the old style, with the second floor out over the first, it's probably old enough.'"

"That would be a fizzing coincidence with what happened to me" I said, "my appendicitis, you, Gillan, and Sam hauling me to Sam's mum in Globe Street."

"Yeah, would be," Zeb said. "They say instead of telling Bytre the truth about his pain, they told him his soul ached from all his wrongdoing and that they would remove it. Suddenly, the pirate ain't so tough. He acts pious and begs them not to take his soul. Just before his hanging, those in charge gauged the drop wrong for Billy's weight. Gillan laughed as he told me, 'The deathsmen must have fancied themselves headsmen, 'cause Billy's head popped off when he reached the end of his rope.' He said it bounced into the crowd of onlookers standing on the foreshore, snapping and biting as it went. Took a chunk out of a young woman's arm, then the thumb of a man who tried to overpower it. The man is bleeding, but he gets it face down on the foreshore and calls for a shovel. They dig a hole, and drop the head in. It keeps bouncing around in there, snapping and biting. Someone finds a broken door among the junk what's collected around the pilings of the dock. They haul that over and put it on top of the hole and heap more gravel and mud on it. They think that will silence the pirate since crushing 'neath a door is one way the law has punished witches."

"They used to execute witches that way," I said, "not trap them."

"Frightened people do all sorts of odd things," Zeb said. "Must have worked, though, 'cause that's the end of the tale, so I'd guess Bytre's head is still there. Buried about four feet down, it's not likely the head made it's way to the surface for me to find. Gillan said they hacked up the rest of Billy and threw the pieces in the river."

"Unlock a *door* in the fore*shore*," I sang, remembering my words on the day we found the black doorknob and Sam cut his foot on the skull's teeth. "On the skull you dug up, had the teeth been sharpened?"

"No." Zeb said.

"Then it must not be his."

"Right. One last bit about Bytre—that young woman with the chunk out of her arm, she were the caretaker for her grandmother, a woman gone barmy from old age. The girl bit the nose and ears off her. The old woman died of her wounds while in the Lambeth Workhouse infirmary. The young woman ended her days in Bedlam."

"In a story that old, it's hard to tell what's true and what's added to make a better tale of it," I said.

He nodded. "Still, from a pirate what bites, you might get a worse infection."

I had to wonder if that could be true. After she took out my appendix, Margaret talked about the danger of something she called germs and the need to keep the wound clean to prevent infection. "I boiled all the tools used in your surgery, so I wouldn't leave germs inside your gut. Because they cannot be seen by the naked eye, many don't believe in them. Some of those who don't believe are physicians. The *Fools*." She explained that, to see germs, you need a certain type of eye piece. Or maybe it were a machine of some sort she described.

Since I had healed up fine, I decided she had the problem well in hand. I set aside my worry, at least for a time, satisfied I'd done what I could to look out for Sam. His mum, witch or not, would surely take care of him.

When he had not returned to the streets after two months, I might have knocked on Margaret Sutton's door myself, yet I didn't want to tempt her to send another demander to threaten me. The first one were no longer a threat, thanks to Bart, may his soul rest in peace. I am ashamed to admit that I let my fear of her keep me from looking in on Sam.

After three months, I worried Sam had become deathly ill or she'd sent him somewheres. I had to go find out.

My knock on Margaret Sutton's door went unanswered. I tried the old servants entrance to the area below. The door had been locked and I got no answer to my knock there. I returned to her house several days in a row, knocking and calling out for both Sam and Margaret. I listened with my ear to the front door and the area door each time, and heard nothing from within.

A big cove—a lumper by the looks of him—challenged me on the third day. "Look here, young man," says he, "I have no reason to protect Miss Sutton, but should you be working yourself up to house-breaking, that's another thing."

"No, sir," I said. "I'm Rollo. I'm looking for her son, Sam, a friend of mine. Have you seen him?"

"I knew him once when he were just a nipper," the cove said, "Used to allow him a puff or two on my pipe. I haven't seen him hereabouts in a couple of years. If I see the Sutton woman, I'll tell her Rollo is looking for Sam."

I couldn't decide whether or not I liked that idea, but I kept my thoughts to myself except to say, "Thank you, sir."

I moved on to knock on the doors of some of Margaret's neighbors. The only answer I got came from an elderly woman, Mrs. Zovko, at the house just to the west.

As she opened her door, the reek of burnt hair from inside took my breath away. I choked, then coughed, trying to clear my pipes before speaking. I'd yet to say anything when she spoke up in a heavy European accent. "My hearing suffers from years working in a saw mill. You'll have to speak up." She cupped a hand behind an ear.

I shouted my questions a few times before she made out what I was saying.

"What does Sam look like?" Mrs. Zovko asked. She glanced back into her house as if remembering something she needed to take care of right away.

"He's a bit shorter than I am, maybe five feet tall, six or seven stone, dark curly hair, round, red-cheeked face."

"Sounds like any of a number of young tearaways I've seen lately," she said, almost at a whisper. Mrs. Zovko looked me up and down, perhaps taking a dim view of me as well.

"And Miss Sutton—have you seen her?"

"Not that I'd want to, but I did see someone looked a lot like her over in Trinity Square." Another glance back and she said, "I have to get back to my cooking."

The notion that she would eat whatever had made that smell turned my stomach. I thanked her and hurried away.

At Trinity Square, a busy, noisy place with many people milling about, I took my time looking for Margaret. I described her to a couple of buskers I knew—a man, Jacob Wertheimer, and his wife, Ludmila— even as they performed their juggling act. No luck. They had not seen her. I decided to go back each day.

In the small hours of the night, I broke into Miss Sutton's house. Surprised to have difficulty with the lock—it were better quality than most, resisting my betty's light touch. Almost broke her off in the key-hole before the latch clicked open.

Inside, the place smelled like a musty attic what had not been opened for a long time. The rooms looked cluttered, not unclean. I found some of Margaret's personal things, clothing and the like, and some medical stuff. An odd heavy garment with helmet, like a suit of armor made of leather, hung in a wardrobe in what must have been her bedroom. Also, I found a curious thing in the padded room where I'd once healed up: the latch with the black doorknob Sam had taken from the foreshore and installed on Bart's door in the house in Pennington Street—the one we discovered again later on the foreshore after the house collapsed and got thrown in the river. The thing lay on the floor next to the open door, Sam's Jacket beside it. Looking closer, I saw dried blood and a bit of gray hair clinging to the big black knob. Margaret's hair? I couldn't make sense of it.

The latch and knob looked to be the only sign Sam had been there. Downstairs in the kitchen, the old-fashioned, deep firebox, once used for cooking, were full of ashes, as though rubbish, mostly paper and cloth, had been dumped into hot coals. Stirring the ash, I saw burnt bones.

Perhaps another sign of Sam? Had Margaret killed him and burned his corpse? Not wanting that to be true, I decided that not enough of the cracked and broken shards remained in the firebox to form the skeleton of a young man, even one small as Sam. The largest pieces might have come from roasted joints of gammon or mutton. Why burn them when the bone grubber would gladly take them away?

I would get nowhere with such questions, I decided, and left, taking the door latch with me. Before returning to our house beside the Shadwell rail station, I threw the latch into the river, watched as it spun through the air, sunlight flashing off the big black knob before it struck the water.

Arriving home, I found that Zeb and Gillan were out, which saved me a lot of explaining. They likely wondered why I hadn't been around much. We'd been considering a bit of the "what if" having to do with a strongbox I'd spied being hauled from a Royal Mail Ship into a warehouse office in Poplar. All that stood between us and that box: two night rounders and the padlock on the office door. We may well have missed our chance at it anyway—conditions for such thefts most often don't last long. Yes, they would have questions I couldn't answer easily.

I retrieved plenty of coin and soft from my hiding place and left, not knowing when I'd return.

With Sam never far from my thoughts, I moved through the following days and weeks. Dipping and hoisting and selling the swag to my fence kept me in coin, as I broadened my search for Sam and Margaret in all directions, south of the river as well. I might have had Gillan and Zeb help me, but I knew they'd hold me back. I moved faster and covered more ground without them.

I couldn't see Margaret going far from where her practice had a good reputation. If what Sam had said bore out, far fewer of her clientele ended up dead than those of other abortionists. He said that, despite the way others saw Margaret, her abilities as a barber surgeon had been rarely questioned. Perhaps that were in part because she only helped single women, she allowed them time to recover in the Globe Street house, and she disposed of her few failures in the river before anyone found out about them. This last, I also had from Sam, who didn't mind airing his mother's dirty laundry with me.

Even knowing she pursued an illegal trade, the mutton shunters turned a blind eye to Margaret Sutton. She either paid them off or they'd decided on their own not to hinder one who reduced the numbers of unwanted children among the poor and destitute, thus reducing the amount of crime we got up to. Yes, though eighteen years old at the time of my search for the Suttons, I counted myself among the unwanted because I'd grown up a hungry, homeless, thieving nipper.

With all that, I didn't blame the poor for the city's woes, and I wouldn't have anyone mistake my words as praise for the police. The blue bottles had once beaten me to satisfy a merchant who mistook me for the thief who robbed his shop. They had no proof and saw no need for it.

On another occasion, they locked me up for several days because someone said the "fine wirer" what robbed them looked like me. I didn't mind being thought of as a highly skilled pickpocket, but again, they had the wrong man.

Although they blinked when it came to those offering a priceless, if unlawful, service like abortion, the way the mutton shunters had treated me in the past, I preferred to give them nothing.

To be expected, outside of a part of Wapping, none knew Sam. And though some got a knowing look as I asked about her, none admitted the slightest acquaintance with Margaret Sutton. A few of the men I tried to question ran me off, as if, merely saying her name, I were indeed conjuring the witch. A big cove tried to punch me in the face. I dodged and ran for it. He didn't chase me.

For more than a month, I looked for the Suttons through the streets, markets, parks, churchyards, and graveyards. I visited casual wards, infirmaries, and hospitals. I made my rounds of her house, and Trinity Square. How many times I got asked to leave pubs and taverns for not ordering food or drink, I cannot say. I'd got so bent on my search, I did not notice dippers robbing me on three different occasions. Since I'd gained what they took by that selfsame method, I could hardly complain.

I walked so far on those stone lanes, my ratty shoes give out and my feet felt miserable. Chill fall weather while in Houndsditch urged me to hoist a pair from a shoe vamper's coster bench at the Rag Fair. I made a weekly trek to that market to see my fence and unload my harvest of mostly sneezers and onions, what most called handkerchiefs and watches. Feeling plumper in the pocket and wearing my new crab-shells, I walked on into the winter, asking after Sam and Margaret Sutton with countless strangers where ever I went.

In mid-December, at the opening to a back lane near the Liverpool Railway Station, I saw a woman crouched down on the pavers, gnawing on what looked like a chicken bone. Precious little on it but gristle. Still, she were making a go at it with the teeth on the right side of her mouth, her breath in the chill air like smoke rising from a furiously working engine.

Something about those teeth looked wrong, yet with the movement I couldn't quite make out what. She bit the end off the bone, sucked out its marrow, and dropped it. Several more bones, picked clean and lying at her feet, seemed to have come from a refuse bin behind her, what might have belonged to the Horns Pub, which backed onto the alley. I saw no teeth on the left side of her mouth and the angry red flesh of her cheek and lips on that side looked to have partly healed from a recent wound. Farther up, also on the left side of her head, she had another red wound not quite healed, showing through her hair above the ear. Her hair there were matted with dried blood, forming a great scab and reminding me of what I'd seen on the black doorknob. Yes, though matted and bedraggled, the hair could have belong to Margaret. She cut her eyes at me and growled like a vicious animal when I got too close, again releasing a big, white cloud into the cold air.

Her togs, green patterned skirt, matching bodice, and a faded blue and green shawl, had been familiar. That's why I'd stopped. But I'd never seen them in such sad shape, torn and stained. Her head had been poked through a large hole in her shawl.

I crouched down to look her in the face and she scuttled back into shadows in the alley, upsetting the refuse bin and an empty barrel. Quick as it had been, I'd got a glimpse of her full face. She were indeed Margaret Sutton, brought low.

As hungry as all that, I told myself, *she might tolerate my presence for a short while, should I feed her.* "Margaret, shall I get you something to eat?"

She glanced up upon hearing her name. Yes, this had been Margaret Sutton. Still, I got the oddest feeling I looked at her twin, one with a different manner and temperament about her. She nodded and I reached out a hand to help her stand. She gave my hand a chary look, then slowly reached out and took it, squeezing too hard. As I helped her up, she wrapped her arms around me and leaned in like she wanted to kiss me. She reeked of rubbish, sweat, and piss. Instead of a kiss, she tried to bite my lip. Quick, I pushed her away and she stood on wobbly legs chuckling. The teeth she had left in her mouth had been ground to sharp points. A good thing I'd acted fast. I thought of Billy the Biter and his cutthroats storming the deck of an enemy ship. How the hell had she done that to her teeth? I imagined her going at them with a hammer and chisel and maybe a file.

She allowed me to take her arm and we walked into the railway station. At the Half Moon Tavern within, I knew I could get her something to eat at a price not too dear. People who saw us stared at her. She'd stare them down before turning away.

At the entrance to the tavern, a plump gentleman in a checked blue and brown suit looked us over, his eyes squinted up like he'd had a hard day and we were making it harder still. "You can't bring her in here," he says. "Not like that."

"Pipe-spit and black toenails," Margaret said, and tried to turn around to leave.

I held on. "My mother doesn't have much," I told him, "but I have plenty. She has suffered an injury and needs to eat to keep her strength. Should you turn us away, I'll take her to one of the pubs across the lane."

"She stinks and her wound is ugly enough to spoil appetites. That's not good for business. Take her to hospital."

"I will as soon as she gets something to eat."

A pub would be noisy, and I feared Margaret, as troubled as she seemed to be, would not do well in that sort of spot. I pulled out a purse I'd freed from a gentleman not ten minutes before I spotted Margaret. I hadn't had the chance to look inside. By the weight, feel, and sound of it, there were at least a couple of pounds in pence and shillings inside. "A private box, perhaps." I pulled two shillings from the purse and offered them to him.

He nodded, and led the way through a back passage to a drinking box toward the rear of the establishment.

"A cold chop, bread, and beer for each of us," I said.

"Tell the Lady of the Napkins," he said with a huff and departed.

Margaret pulled the shawl off and sat. I took my coat off, gathered up her shawl, and hung both on hooks beside the exit to the box before taking a seat.

"How did you suffer such harm to your head?" I asked.

But for a quick glance at me, she kept her head down. "Food," she said, smacking her lips and drooling a bit. Like petting a beloved animal, her hands explored the table top. She wiggled in her chair as if testing it, then leaned it back against the wall so she could recline, a look of satisfaction on her face. She spread her legs as a man might do, her filthy lower legs and ratty shoes exposed beneath the hem of her skirts as she rested her feet on the chair's cross-stretcher.

I asked my question again.

"Sam," she said.

A barmaid knocked on the entrance to the box, and leaned in. Seeing Margaret, her eyes got large, yet she kept her thoughts to herself. I made my request for food and drink, and she left.

"Yes, where is Sam?" I asked.

"He did this." Margaret reached to touch the wound on the left side of her head and winced. She then touched her damaged cheek more carefully.

I decided Sam must have had his reasons. He were not the violent sort, not without good reason.

"Margaret…," I started and she looked up at me as though I'd just sat down. "…where is he? Where is Sam?"

"Oh, Rollo," She dropped the front legs of her chair and sat upright. Her eyes wide and pained, her crooked mouth pinched, she said most pitifully, "help me, please."

"I will help you. I *am* helping you."

"Help me before they come back," Margaret said. She glanced about, looking a bit confused, the flesh around her right eye twitching.

"Who?"

Her expression changed, the right side of her face grew calm, the gaze of that eye becoming steady, as she regarded me. "Clever lad, he used a piece of my tooth and done like I asked. Now he's in the river, poor fellow."

"What did you ask him to do?"

She didn't answer. Only chomped her sharp teeth at me, as if to bite.

Had she done as I'd feared? No, she didn't make sense. Margaret Sutton had gone as mad as her crazy Uncle Geoffrey.

"When he done it," she said, "she stabbed him in the gut. He had his jacket with something heavy in it." She gestured toward her two wounds as though striking them hard, and jerking her head to the right each time, like taking blows.

"Where is Sam now?"

"I told you, in the river. She got him in the neck too. He grew weak quickly. And though she'd been grievous harmed, she had him to pieces in her scullery. Several went into the river that night, others burned. I were too small yet to help, to stop her. I'm sorry. I've grown since."

"Did you kill Sam?"

"Not me, hobbadehoy."

A lunatic or not, I'd lost all pity for her. I believed she and Sam had fought and she'd killed him and dumped him in the river, the same as he'd told me she'd done to the women who died in her care. That made sense, whilst she did not. She didn't even sound like herself. If anything, she sounded like one from the street, her manner that of a rough cove as she leaned back in her chair again.

One of the waitstaff brought our food.

I got up to leave. I could not eat with such a monster.

She dropped the front legs of her chair, leaned forward, and went at the food like a starving beast.

"Margaret," I said. "You've got what you deserve."

She paused and looked up at me with a lopsided smile. "If you please, sir, call me Elizabeth," she said, and carried on with her eating.

A middle name or just more madness?

I turned away and left the premises. Short of killing her, I could think of nothing worse for one who hated the poor like Margaret did than to be off her chump on the pitiless streets of London. Let her suffer, I thought.

But on my way home, I got the oddest feeling I had mistaken someone else for Margaret Sutton. I kept picturing her jagged smile and wondering if a truth were hidden behind it. Aside from not making sense, her words troubled me—where had her proper English gone?

Did Billy the Biter somehow figure into this, and, if so, how? Zeb had said that the girl on the foreshore, what the skull had bitten during Bytre's hanging, had gone on to bite her grandmother, killing her. I didn't believe in ghosts, much less in possession of the living by the dead. Even so, might that have explained what had happened to Margaret Sutton? And then there were the many coincidences what begged for answers: the pirate's prostitutes hacked up and the few women Margaret had lost over the years cut up and dumped in the river; a barber surgeon in Wapping tending appendicitis, mine and William Bytre's; the teeth ground to points, the pirate's and Margaret's; The skull Zeb discovered and the tale about the pirate's head being buried in the same stretch of foreshore; the doorknob and latch found three times, twice in the river and once in the house in Globe Street; the damaged left feet, Sam's, Bart's, and Dog Face Dowd's. And there were more.

Though I had plenty of questions, no ready answers came.

Thereafter, I left off with my search for Sam. I never saw him again, never met anyone who had seen him after he went missing. I also never again saw Margaret, or the woman calling herself Elizabeth.

Over time, thinking about those poor women Margaret Sutton had killed, and Sam as well, I gained a fear of finding a watery grave what held something with the flesh still on it. I gave up mudlarking. I do miss receiving the occasional rewards Father Thames offers.

Life goes on. Zeb and I are now employed at the Billingsgate Fish Market as porters. My sweetheart, Maple, and I will be wed within the month, and I've secured lodgings for us in a nice house in Poplar. Gillan will stand as my best man. He redeemed himself, defending me against three fellows trying to roll me in the very alley off Brewhouse Lane where I'd tried to give Sam a dewskitch.

Another mysterious coincidence? Could be. I am not as curious about them as I'd once been. And whilst they niggle at me daily, I have come to terms with not having answers to my questions.

I do sorely miss Sam.

32-Samuel
The Thames foreshore, Wapping, London
1906

My head, a vessel holding all that's left of me, is submerged, bits and pieces of rubbish pinning it to the river bed in the shallows. Somehow, this watery realm is familiar.

A dream? Perhaps, yet I also carry a dread more persuasive than what may come in dreams.

Although I don't know why, I find myself comparing my plight to that of a captain whose ship at sea pirates have stormed and scuttled. Small life plucks at me and I have no way to fight back. I am rudderless and am made smaller by the day.

My thoughts seem an echo of someone else's. Memories of her—yes, a woman—are incomplete and come slowly. She took up inside me for a time, but she no longer needs me. And whilst I don't know of what sort, I know she found a path out of her suffering.

I am not alone. Another shares this dismal place with me. He's a very old, enfeebled spirit who relishes violence, even cannibalism. I cannot make much sense of his thoughts.

Do we both suffer a similar fate? I have no answer to that.

On occasion, he seems to be gone—for days, months, years, I cannot say. If he does indeed leave, I don't know how he does or where he goes.

He is here now. That troubles me because, even though he doesn't have the presence the woman did, I feel the grind of his meaningless, angry thoughts and I fear he might take an interest in me. I do not want that anger turned in my direction. And yet, should he know a way out of this watery place, I will want to hear from him.

I'd prefer it be the woman. With that, if she returns, I don't know that she would help me. Memories of her come on at a damnably-slow pace.

Though my sight suffers I see a black doorknob not far away, poking up into the air when the tide goes out. I have the sense that I've known that

135

knob before. Through sheer will alone, I find that I can turn it a little. The threshold it guards could be the path the woman took. Or the door could be all that stands between me and the angry, enfeebled spirit.

Should I get it open, I still cannot move toward it.

Once the door is opened, whatever is beyond the threshold could come for me.

Should he come through, he'll bring his aimless desire for vengeance with him and I'll suffer.

No, such thoughts only discourage. I must get it opened!

I can but try.

Afterword: A Society Overrun with the Destitute and Homeless

Imagine you see someone impoverished on a street corner, perhaps a homeless person. They are part of your society, but you don't owe them anything directly, except perhaps courtesy. Even that is unnecessary if you walk by without interacting. Do that enough, and the impoverished become a distant fact of life, more an inconvenience than anything else. Yet, they have needs that are not being met. Desperation prompts them to do things to get attention. Sometimes those efforts take them from being an inconvenience to being a nuisance. At least to those of us who feel entitled to a comfortable life; that can feel very uncomfortable.

"I don't like the way that person smells."

"Their language is offensive."

"If you let that person get away with it, what else might they do?"

Yet, they are human beings. Some have not served themselves well in life. Some suffer physical or mental handicaps. There are myriad reasons why an individual might not see success in life. I speak the obvious.

Now imagine you are a nineteenth century monarchy with a state-sanctioned religion and a class system. Instead of having a few impoverished people, your society has an underclass numbering a million or more. The class system helps keep the poor powerless, and puts limits on their ambitions, but it doesn't keep them from breeding. And, of course, your state-sanctioned religion requires that you have legislation that makes abortion illegal. This is a recipe for endemic squalor among your citizenry. But to do anything about it would require sacrifices from those with power and wealth; the nobles, the land owners, the industrialists, the legislators, the church.

Do you just walk away?

In Victorian England, most of those with power and wealth did walk away for as long as they thought they could get away with it. Even those who were not well-to-do had little to offer the poor.

"Not my problem."

"The government will take care of it, but they'd better not raise my taxes to do it."

"That's what the workhouse is for."

"I wouldn't have nearly enough to offer to make a dent in the problem, and I need what I've got for myself and my family."

"If you give the homeless a free lunch, they'll never want to pay."

"Why should they get a free ride, when I have to work so hard to earn a crust?

"Since I was capable of earning my wealth, I deserve it, while those who are destitute made their own beds or are constitutionally incapable of organizing themselves for success."

"If they have too many children, the wife must be a wanton woman and the drunkard husband is no model of rectitude. They deserve what they get. Their children will be no better and deserve no consideration."

As the numbers of the poor grew, many parents too impoverished to care for their children took up infanticide as a means of addressing the problem.

The authors of this novel, both citizens of the United States, believe abortion should be an option that is legal, regulated, and safe. Making abortion illegal does not make it go away. Instead, it is returned to those of the underworld, where unregulated, unscrupulous practitioners will perform the service in back alleys in conditions of filth, and provide no after-procedure care. We are returned to a situation in which many women and girls will die from dangerous abortion practices. As a reminder, in the old days, the bent coat hanger came to symbolize the back-alley option.

This novel is, in part, about an abortionist in Victorian London during a time when Great Britain, the richest, most influential, and technologically advanced nation of the period, had some of the worst poverty in the world and a growing problem with infanticide.

—Alan M. Clark & Rebecca Allred
Oregon, United States

About the Authors

Rebecca J. Allred is the author of numerous short stories including "The Dark Wood Teaman," "Once, I Dreamed I was Dead," "Mother's Mouth, Full of Dirt," and "The Last Plague Doctor." Her novella, *And In Her Smile, The World* (written with Gordon B. White) was a finalist for the 2022 Bram Stoker Award®.

Author, illustrator, and publisher, Alan M. Clark, grew up in Tennessee in a house full of bones and old medical books. In his thirty-nine years as a freelance illustrator, he has created illustrations for hundreds of books, including works of fiction of various genres, nonfiction, textbooks, young adult fiction, and children's books. During his twenty-nine years as a freelance writer, he has authored twenty-three published books, including sixteen novels, a lavishly illustrated novella, a lavishly illustrated novelette, four collections of fiction, and a nonfiction full-color book of his artwork. Honors for his work include the World Fantasy Award, four Chesley Awards, and he is an International Book Awards winner. Alan M. Clark and his wife, Melody, live in Oregon.

www.alanmclark.com

IFD Publishing Paperbacks

Novels:

Of Thimble and Threat, by Alan M. Clark
Baggage Check, by Elizabeth Engstrom
Bull's Labyrinth, by Eric Witchey
The Surgeon's Mate: A Dismemoir, by Alan M. Clark
Siren Promised, by Jeremy Robert Johnson and Alan M. Clark
Say Anything but Your Prayers, by Alan M. Clark
Candyland, by Elizabeth Engstrom
Apologies to the Cat's Meat Man, by Alan M. Clark
Lizzie Borden, by Elizabeth Engstrom
A Parliament of Crows, by Alan M. Clark
Lizard Wine, by Elizabeth Engstrom
The Door that Faced West, by Alan M. Clark
The Northwoods Chronicles, by Elizabeth Engstrom
The Prostitute's Price, by Alan M. Clark
The Assassin's Coin, by John Linwood Grant
13 Miller's Court, by Alan M. Clark and John Linwood Grant
Guys Named Bob, by Elizabeth Engstrom
Fallen Giants of the Points, by Alan M. Clark
The Itinerant, by Elizabeth Engstrom
York's Moon, by Elizabeth Engstrom
Night Birds, by Lisa Snellings and Alan M. Clark
The Witch of Wapping, by Rebecca J. Allred and Alan M. Clark

Collections:

Professor Witchey's Miracle Mood Cure, by Eric Witchey

Nonfiction:

How to Write a Sizzling Sex Scene, by Elizabeth Engstrom
Divorce by Grand Canyon, by Elizabeth Engstrom

IFD Publishing EBooks

(You can find the following titles at most distribution points for all
ereading platforms.)

Novels:
The Prostitute's Price, by Alan M. Clark
The Assassin's Coin, by John Linwood Grant
13 Miller's Court, by Alan M. Clark and John Linwood Grant
Guys Named Bob, by Elizabeth Engstrom
Apologies to the Cat's Meat Man, by Alan M. Clark
Bull's Labyrinth, by Eric Witchey
The Surgeon's Mate: A Dismemoir, by Alan M. Clark
York's Moon, by Elizabeth Engstrom
Beyond the Serpent's Heart, by Eric Witchey
Lizzie Borden, by Elizabeth Engstrom
A Parliament of Crows, by Alan M. Clark
Lizard Wine, by Elizabeth Engstrom
Northwoods Chronicles, by Elizabeth Engstrom
Siren Promised, by Alan M. Clark and Jeremy Robert Johnson
To Kill a Common Loon, by Mitch Luckett
The Man in the Loon, by Mitch Luckett
Of Thimble and Threat, by Alan M. Clark
Jack the Ripper Victim Series: The Double Event (includes two novels
from the series: *Of Thimble and Threat* and *Say Anything But Your
Prayers*) by Alan M. Clark
Candyland, by Elizabeth Engstrom
The Blood of Father Time: Book 1, The New Cut, by Alan M. Clark,
Stephen C. Merritt & Lorelei Shannon
The Blood of Father Time: Book 2, The Mystic Clan's Grand Plot, by
Alan M. Clark, Stephen C. Merritt & Lorelei Shannon
*How I Met My Alien Bitch Lover: Book 1 from the Sunny World Inquisi-
tion Daily Letter Archives*, by Eric Witchey
Baggage Check, by Elizabeth Engstrom
D.D. Murphry, Secret Policeman, by Alan M. Clark & Elizabeth
Massie
Black Leather, by Elizabeth Engstrom
Fallen Giants of the Points, by Alan M. Clark
The Itinerant, by Elizabeth Engstrom
Night Birds, by Lisa Snellings and Alan M. Clark
The Witch of Wapping, by Rebecca J. Allred and Alan M. Clark

Novelettes:
Mudlarks and the Silent Highwayman, by Alan M. Clark
The Tao of Flynn, by Eric Witchey
To Build a Boat, Listen to Trees, by Eric Witchey

Children's Illustrated:
The Christmas Thingy, by F. Paul Wilson. Illustrated by Alan M. Clark

Collections:
Suspicions, by Elizabeth Engstrom
Professor Witchey's Miracle Mood Cure, by Eric Witchey

Short Fiction:
"Brittle Bones and Old Rope," by Alan M. Clark
"Crosley," by Elizabeth Engstrom
"The Apple Sniper," by Eric Witchey

Nonfiction:
How to Write a Sizzling Sex Scene, by Elizabeth Engstrom
Divorce by Grand Canyon, by Elizabeth Engstrom

IFD Publishing Audio Books

Novels:
The Door That Faced West by Alan M. Clark, read by Charles Hinckley
Jack the Ripper Victim Series: Of Thimble and Threat, by Alan M. Clark, read by Alicia Rose
Jack the Ripper Victim Series: Say Anything But Your Prayers, by Alan M. Clark, read by Alicia Rose
Jack the Ripper Victim Series: The Double Event, by Alan M. Clark, read by Alicia Rose (includes two novels from the series: *Of Thimble and Threat* and *Say Anything But Your Prayers*)
A Parliament of Crows, by Alan M. Clark, read by Laura Jennings
A Brutal Chill in August, by Alan M. Clark, read by Alicia Rose
The Surgeon's Mate: A Dismemoir, by Alan M. Clark, read by Alan M. Clark
Apologies to the Cat's Meat Man, by Alan M. Clark, read by Alicia Rose

www.ingramcontent.com/pod-product-compliance
Lightning Source LLC
Chambersburg PA
CBHW060425260626
47161CB00005B/1784